PLAYER!

A Walker Brothers Novel

J.S. SCOTT

Player!
A Walker Brothers Novel

Cover Design by Stacey Chappell

ISBN: 978-1-939962-91-1 (E-Book)
ISBN: 978-1-939962-92-8 (Paperback)

CONTENTS

CHAPTER 1

Sebastian

I knew the moment that we both stepped into the elevator on the ground floor of Walker Enterprises that I wanted her—and I didn't even know her name.

It happened just that quickly, my underused dick was as hard as a rock within moments, which hadn't happened at all in the last year or so.

And that reaction got my full attention. It was unusual for me. I just wasn't made that way.

Okay. Yeah. During my party days it was non-stop drinking, getting high, and hot females who wanted to get laid. I have to admit, I definitely accommodated them back then.

But things were different for me now. I took my position at Walker Enterprises seriously, and I'd never been so content with my life as I had during the last year.

I fit.

I belonged.

I felt like I was finally in control of my own damn destiny and individual success.

I had a purpose, and it felt pretty damn good.

I didn't need booze. I didn't need weed. I didn't need...

Oh hell, I couldn't exactly say I didn't need women anymore, but my desire to forge my place in Walker had far exceeded my desire to get laid.

Until now. *Right* now. *This* woman, *this* elevator, and *this* instant hard-on.

It wasn't exactly something I wanted right now—but on the question of whether I *needed* women? My dick was suddenly in control of my brain.

It was morning, the beginning of the workday, and every elevator was packed. I stepped back into the corner next to her so I could inhale her tantalizing, light floral scent. It was subtle—just like her. But she was a female I noticed the minute I was elbow-to-elbow with the first woman who had stirred any kind of lustful interest from my body since I'd moved to Denver from Texas and joined my brother at Walker.

Not that *she* was actually *trying* to get my attention—or any other male glances for that matter. My senses noticed her, even though she seemed to prefer the exact opposite—being invisible. There was something about the fact that I was the only guy who seemed to recognize that underneath that prim, gray pencil skirt, white blouse, and matching jacket was a female worth watching amused me.

She was hiding, haunted about something that made her want distance from the world. I should know. I'd been there.

I sensed that almost immediately. But it didn't matter. For some reason, I could see right through her camouflage and imagine her naked, writhing in ecstasy as I banged her up against the wall of the elevator.

And dammit, I was curious to know exactly what secrets she didn't want anyone to know. She was curvy, but one wouldn't notice from the way her shapeless jacket covered her breasts and the majority of what I already knew was a shapely ass.

Her ebony hair was long, thick and sexy as hell. I could tell from the massive bun that formed behind her head. And damn, she was a stunner who needed very little makeup with her creamy, unblemished skin.

She'd done everything to downplay her physical assets. However, I still seemed to do nothing but fantasize about every single one of them.

I was blatantly staring at her, but she ignored me completely, clutching her briefcase and looking straight ahead, like she never even knew I was standing right next to her.

What the hell? Women had always noticed me, regardless of whether or not I wanted the attention.

Maybe the fact that she didn't acknowledge my presence was what really had my cock trying to burst through the crotch of my pants. I was operating on a primitive level at the moment, and damned if I didn't want to give chase and conquer her, *make* her notice me.

She was different, and I liked that. Her attention was focused on something far more important to her than anybody who was riding the elevator at the moment.

What is she thinking about?

Her behavior certainly had me interested to know where her brain was at right now, because she definitely didn't seem to be surveying the people around her.

I get that most people try not to *appear* like they're checking out their fellow passengers; it's something we do covertly. But not her. She was entirely in her own universe.

I watched as people filtered out every time the elevator stopped while we slowly crawled to the top of the building. The lift halted at every floor as we crept toward the last few stops, which were all executive offices.

I knew this because *my* office is on the very top floor.

Let me be quite honest and admit that it had been a while since a woman had entirely discounted my presence. Especially when they found out that I was Sebastian Walker, co-owner and billionaire partner—along with my brother, Trace—of Walker Enterprises.

I acknowledged that without conceit. It's just fact. When a guy has as much money as I do, and hasn't yet hit the age of thirty, most women looked at me as a potential, eligible male. It's been happening since I turned eighteen, almost ten years ago.

However, since I've now worked at Walker with my brother, Trace, for nearly a year, most of the females who worked in our main offices here in Denver knew my reputation—or maybe I should say my *past* behavior. It caused many of them to keep their distance, which was fine with me.

Honestly, I think the ones who didn't try to snag me anymore were pretty smart. I wasn't exactly a relationship type of guy.

I was a player, the party guy who had never taken work seriously until I had to man up and put my money into this business with Trace. Now that I had bought back into my deceased father's corporation, I was fully committed, dedicated heart and soul to Walker. Unfortunately, my reputation preceded me, and very few people had yet to figure out that I was now reformed.

Well…okay…maybe *reformed* wasn't exactly the right word to sum up my transformation. I'm still the same rich guy who has never seen poverty, and really doesn't know what it's like to be a normal person. But I gave up getting high, and being a professional partier. Hell, I very rarely even had a drink anymore, which makes me downright boring to many women. But I'm too damn busy, which is exactly why I'm really *not* a player anymore. During the last year or so, not a single woman has pulled my interest away from business since I'd partnered in Walker with Trace…*until* today.

I had to prove myself, carve out my place in the company, but I was good with that. I had a purpose, and it was to be an asset to Walker, and take some of the load off my elder brother, Trace. I also wanted to carve out my own niche in the company and become a valuable asset to the conglomerate.

Trace had finally settled down and gotten married to a woman who really loved him. Eva had been the best thing that ever happened to my older sibling, and he deserved to slow his ass down for a while.

Luckily, I'd also become obsessed with my job, which meant I didn't miss my days of being high and drunk. *Okay. Yeah.* Maybe I *did* miss getting laid more often, but I hadn't really thought about it until *she* walked into the same elevator as me this morning. My dick was now in an all-out revolt from lack of use, and I had to loosen the tie on my custom, power suit because the small space was getting warm, even though people were filing out on every floor.

"Would you mind moving over?" the woman suddenly asked politely, but firmly, as she put an elbow lightly into my ribs.

Damn! Her voice was just as serious as her old-lady suit. But it was a husky alto that sounded pretty fucking sexy, even if she *was* shrugging me off.

Maybe I *was* a little too close to her—considering we were the last ones left in the lift.

I moved to the other side of our small space, able to watch her better as I leaned against the opposite wall. "Still going up?"

"Yes," she answered brusquely, finally looking over at me with a pair of beautiful blue eyes that were almost completely devoid of emotion, and as cool as a winter's day in Colorado.

She didn't give me flirtatious looks.

She didn't appear to check me out.

If anything, she may have had a brief flash of loathing before she wiped any semblance of emotion from her face.

Her lack of expression didn't surprise me. I was fairly certain *the look* came from plenty of practice.

There wasn't a whole lot left above this floor except the executive offices. I had to wonder where she was going. "You work here?"

She shot me a glance that inferred that I was asking a stupid question. Maybe it was a little ignorant since the whole building belonged to Walker, and she most definitely looked like she was on her way to work.

"Yes. First day here," she answered blandly.

She certainly wasn't chatty, but I'd already suspected that.

"Ah. That's why I don't know you." I shot her my most charming smile, one I hadn't used in quite some time. "Sebastian Walker," I said politely, and held out my hand.

For some sad, unknown reason, I wanted her to be impressed that I was one of the two owners of Walker Enterprises.

She hesitated before she placed her delicate fingers in mine and shook firmly as she replied in a professional tone, "I recognized you from your picture in the lobby. Paige Rutledge. And I'm sure it would be impossible for you to be acquainted with every employee in the building."

No, I wasn't. It actually would be impossible for me to know every soul who worked here at Walker. But I at least knew most of the faces I saw often, which was pretty much the people on the upper floors.

"You're somebody's executive secretary?" Judging by the bland suit and sensible shoes, she looked like a new hire trying to impress her boss.

She snorted. "Not exactly."

I grinned, liking her spunky attitude and mysterious demeanor. My eyes darted to the two floors still lit up on the panel. The top floor was mine. The other had offices right beneath the penthouse floor. "Legal?"

Hell, she had to be a legal secretary. I hadn't quite reached my twenty-eighth birthday, and even though she had the composure and style of someone older, she didn't look a day over twenty-five.

"Yes," she confirmed, not adding anything further.

"Legal secretary." I nodded, knowing I had to be right. We had an entire floor made up of lawyers and their clerical staff.

Her eyes met mine, and I was startled by the disapproval in her gaze. Paige moved forward as the elevator stopped on her floor. When the doors swung open, she exited. Without turning around, she answered my question. "Wrong, Mr. Walker. I'm the new attorney," she answered haughtily, her wool-clad hips swaying slightly as she moved away from the elevator.

I watched her as she neared her offices until the metal doors slammed shut in front of my face.

"She never even turned around," I said to myself in a puzzled tone. "What person does that when they're in the presence of one of the two top guys in their new company?"

In truth, I wasn't pissed off. I was intrigued, and her behavior brought up more questions than answers for me. Paige Rutledge looked focused, determined, and ready to conquer the world. She didn't think she needed to impress me by fawning all over me. She'd been coolly polite, but definitely disinterested. I hadn't been the one who had hired her. Dan Hurst, the Chief Council of the company, did his own hiring. Trace and I left the hiring to the department heads unless they were our executives.

I tried to forget thinking about the strange encounter as my dick started to deflate. Her scent lingered in my memory, but I determinedly tried to switch my mindset to work mode.

My mood changed as I exited on the floor where Trace and I had our offices. I felt the same burst of energy as I'd been feeling for over a year, every time I walked into the executive suites, my mind shifting to my projects.

Since I was an engineer by education, and a businessman by nature, I was pretty excited about the alternative energy projects we were beginning to collect and build. Solar and wind energy had always been my passion, and I was finally able to put my skills to work in a big way. Walker hadn't done much in those progressive fields before I got here, but I was determined to put us over the top in technology and manufacturing. The U.S. was behind other countries on solar, and in my opinion, we should be leading the pack. We had so many untapped resources that would create so many jobs, it seemed almost criminal that we hadn't developed our technology and taken over as the leader in the industry. Untapped resources that were infinite, and we weren't leading the way to being energy independent?

Damn shame.

But I was going to change all that over time. During the last year, my gut hadn't steered me wrong, and Walker was slowly becoming even wealthier than it had been a year ago.

It had taken a lot of investment and trust from my brother and partner to get our alternative energy division moving, and I was determined not to make him regret the changes I'd talked him into. So far, he didn't.

I was surprised when I passed Trace's office and he was already behind his desk. These days, he came in late, probably because he had a loving wife that made him reluctant to get out of bed.

I didn't have that particular issue. I shot out of bed every single morning, ready to start another work day. Part of my job was to acquire solar properties for technology, manufacturing, and massive solar farms. Right now, I was planning one of the largest solar operations in the country, but I'd run into a wall on getting the thousands of acres of property I wanted to collect, manufacture, and develop even better technology. This particular company facility required a lot of space in a sunny area, and I had the perfect location. I just needed to convince the buyer to sell at a reasonable price. Problem was, I was pretty sure he knew what I was doing, and he wanted a piece of the future profits.

Ducking quickly into Trace's office, I said jokingly, "You're here already? Eva must have abandoned you early this morning."

Trace look up from his computer and grinned sheepishly. "She had an eight o'clock class."

Trace's wife was now in culinary school, and kicking ass. She was already an amazing cook. I could only imagine what she would turn out once she finished her formal training. "Must have been rough," I answered with very little sympathy.

So what if he missed his morning wakeup sex.

My brother was rarely early to work anymore, and the bastard probably got some action nearly every damn morning. I assumed more than once a day by the sense of humor he'd developed lately. My poor dick hadn't seen the light of day—other than when I was alone in the shower—for well over a year. I *didn't* feel sorry for Trace because he missed out this morning. One morning wasn't going to kill him. I wanted him to be happy, but damn, it wasn't like he was deprived.

"It *was* rough," Trace grumbled good-naturedly. "But Eva is loving her courses, so I guess I'll live."

I dropped into a comfortable chair in front of his desk. "I think you'll make it until tonight." *Jesus!* He'd see his woman later today. While I was glad he was in love with the right woman, and I adored Eva, my brother was more than a little obsessed with his wife.

"How's the New Mexico project going?" Trace asked as he leaned back in his chair, his dark eyes now focused on me.

"In a holding pattern. I should get some word today whether or not our offer was accepted." I was more than a little excited at the thought of getting the property at a reasonable price so we could start building all we had planned for the site.

Trace shook his head as he locked his hands behind his neck. "I still can't get over how much you've changed. You never told me that you were doing research on alternative energy, or how much you loved solar and wind technology."

It wasn't the first time my older brother had brought up this particular subject. I usually brushed it off. Today, I didn't. "Hell, I couldn't spend every hour of the day getting high. I haven't changed all that much. Yeah, I don't drink much, and quitting the weed wasn't all that difficult. I've always wanted to know where I belonged. It just took me a while to get here."

"Why didn't you ever tell me about the research you were doing between parties?"

I shrugged. "Would it have mattered? I was still fucked up."

"It would have made a difference to me," Trace answered emphatically. "We could have figured everything out sooner."

"I wasn't ready," I insisted. "I had to grow the fuck up."

"I held you back," Trace suggested remorsefully. "I should have questioned what you wanted before I settled Dad's estate."

"It wasn't your fault," I answered honestly. In no way was my previous lifestyle Trace's responsibility. He'd been young—really young—when he'd taken over Walker after my father's untimely death. I had still been in college. I didn't know back then what I wanted myself. By the time he'd separated our father's assets, I was a billionaire before I'd even graduated. In my grief over losing our dad so young to a plane crash, and my younger brother Dane's near escape from death, I'd been a coward, escaping into alcohol and endless parties after college. By the time I discovered that I didn't want a pity-party-for-one, I'd already joined a crowd of other rich and useless people. Living that way had quickly gotten old, but Trace had been running Walker, and I didn't know where I fit in.

Now, I knew.

I was able to apply all the work I'd done alone, pour my efforts into making a difference instead of being a loser who knew a hell of a lot about solar and wind energy, but wasn't doing a damn thing to contribute to bettering the world with my research.

"This company was Dad's. We should have always been partners," Trace insisted. "I know Dane doesn't want any part of it, but I should have waited for you to make a decision after school. You could have added so much from the very beginning. I didn't know shit about that type of technology, and we were making so much money in other ventures that I didn't bother to learn. You're right. It is the future. Walker needed to step into future growth."

"I told you I didn't care," I replied. Back when Trace had needed to settle my dad's estate, I was still in school, and so devastated because my last parent was dead that I was almost numb.

"I shouldn't have believed a damn word you said. We were all in a state of shock. You were young—"

"Like you were so much older?" I leaned back in my chair with a smirk. Trace hadn't even completely finished school himself. He'd had to complete his MBA while he ran the company and settled Dad's estate.

Trace smiled back at me. "I guess we'll have to grow together. I've learned a lot from you already about looking at future technology. I am sorry, Sebastian. It's good to have you here in Denver. And your talent is invaluable."

He'd missed me, just like I'd missed him. I liked Colorado. Although it had been difficult to sell my father's estate and other interests in Texas, I'd liquidated my assets to buy back into Walker, where I belonged.

I'd become too isolated and numb after my dad had died. I hadn't realized how important my family was to me. My brothers were really all I had. The rich party scene had been an illusion, one that had gotten empty and put me into a downward spiral fast.

I owed my brother for hauling me back into the real world. It was a debt I knew I could never repay. My days were busy but useful. I liked that more than I ever could have imagined.

I shrugged. "I love what I'm doing here, and we don't step on each other's toes."

Trace had never had any interest in doing what I was doing, although he asked questions and picked up on where we needed to go pretty quickly. We worked in different areas, which suited both of us just fine.

"You work too much," Trace observed. "How late were you here last night?"

I'd been in the office until well after midnight, obsessed with making a good deal on the New Mexico property. "Not that late," I dismissed.

"Bullshit," Trace answered bluntly. "I called your place at nine, and you didn't answer."

"Maybe I had a date."

"You didn't. Hell, you haven't gone out enough in Denver to even meet anyone."

"I could have been screwing a hot secretary from the fourth floor," I joked, then suddenly remembered the one female who had actually gotten me hard at first sight this morning. "I met the new female attorney in the elevator this morning."

"We have a new one?" Trace questioned.

I wasn't surprised that he didn't know. People got hired and fired in the company all the time without us ever knowing. "Yeah. She looks like jailbait. Her name is Paige Rutledge. I can't believe she's old enough to be an attorney. Maybe she was bull-shitting me."

Trace leaned forward and started typing on the computer, focused on finding what he wanted before he answered. "She's going to turn twenty-seven in a month. Graduated early from high school and had her bachelor's degree in three years. Went directly to law school at Harvard after that." He hesitated as he read something on the screen. "She has some pretty impressive recommendations."

"So she's brilliant, too," I said unhappily. Maybe I'd secretly been hoping she was a fraud so my dick didn't get hard every time I thought about her.

"Too?" Trace lifted an eyebrow suspiciously. "She must be hot," he concluded.

For some reason, I didn't really want to talk about Paige. Honestly, I wanted to forget my body's odd reaction to her. "She's attractive, but not in an obvious way. Would have completely ignored me if I hadn't talked to her first."

"Ouch! Was that painful? First time you've been ignored?" Trace said in a mocking tone.

"It was weird. You know how women usually react when we're around."

"I'm off the market. The female employees respect that. But yeah, even the male employees try to be overly friendly."

"She asked me to give her some space in the elevator," I admitted.

Trace grinned. "Maybe she isn't into men."

I shook my head. "I don't think that's the problem." I could feel some weird chemistry between Paige and me. I was willing to acknowledge it. Sadly, she wasn't.

"She got to you," Trace concluded. "Seriously, maybe she's married or involved?"

"No ring." In fact, I hadn't noticed jewelry of any kind on her body except for a pair of tiny studs in her ears. "I don't think so, but I don't know for sure. No, she didn't get to me," I denied, lying to both my brother and myself. "I just think her behavior was weird for a new employee. They're usually overanxious about making a good impression. Hell, she didn't even smile."

"Maybe she was nervous."

Remembering her curvy, swaying hips and confident tone, I finally answered, "Nope. She sounded perfectly controlled."

"I think maybe I need to go down to the legal department later and check out the new employee who got you thinking about something other than our company," Trace mused. "You haven't talked about women since you moved to Denver."

"No! Forget it. She's just a junior attorney. Not worth your time." I didn't want Paige being nice to Trace when she hadn't been nice to me. It was juvenile, but I was just that covetous of Paige's attention, and I didn't even know her. *Jesus!* I tried to think of the last time I'd been jealous, but I couldn't remember a single woman in my life who I'd wanted to keep all to myself. Honestly, she might react to Trace the same way she did to me.

But I had a feeling she wouldn't. That was the moment when I had to admit to myself that maybe she just thought I was a dick.

Trace was my brother, and completely devoted to his wife, but the thought of Paige being more cordial to my brother than she was to me really did annoy me for some reason.

It was probably the fact that she'd definitely have more respect for Trace than she had for me, the ex-player and spoiled rich brat. I had no doubt that she'd probably heard about both of us during her employee orientation and pre-screening. If she hadn't heard the rumors there, I certainly had made no secret of my past. I'm sure I'd been an embarrassment to Trace more than once when the tales had gone public.

"She has your nuts in a vise," Trace joked.

"I think I need to get laid," I confessed. "It's been over a year. I guess I'm just starting to notice."

"Over a year must be some kind of record for you. Maybe you need to start dating."

It *was* a record, but I didn't tell Trace that he was right. I had screwed around a lot during my party years, deliberately seeking out other rich party girls who just wanted the same thing I wanted. Mostly, I'd forgotten all about the women I'd had. I was usually too hung over and miserable to remember. "I've been busy," I told him defensively.

"Too busy," my brother admonished. "Find a good woman and get laid as often as possible. I highly recommend it."

He would. Trace had a great life now, and Eva to run home to every night. I didn't even have a dog. All that greeted me when I came home was the sound of complete silence.

"I might start thinking about it." My answer was non-committal. I stood up so I could get to my office. "Right now, I need to get to work."

"Sebastian?" Trace summoned as I was ready to walk out the door.

I turned. "Yeah?"

"When you meet the right woman, you'll know it. If I had been honest with myself earlier, I would have admitted I pretty much knew that Eva was going to be the one who sent me over the edge soon after I met her."

No woman was *ever* going to make me as crazy as Trace had been. Our makeup was completely different. I didn't get insanely jealous, or even give a shit who else a woman was fucking. I wasn't made that way. "Hasn't happened yet," I told him as I walked out of his office.

"I said the same thing. I wasn't the kind of guy to fall hard for a woman. It had never happened. But I hadn't met Eva. Be careful what you say. It might just sneak up on you one day."

I knew he was talking about being in love, something I'd never experienced and was pretty convinced didn't exist. I was a science guy. No way was I inclined to think that there was just one woman out there who could make me happy. The world had over seven billion humans, which made the possibility that I'd meet that one woman who supposedly existed only for me pretty damn slim.

Not that I was concerned about meeting a woman and falling in love. I wasn't. I was perfectly content being single.

Since I'd grown up and stopped my senseless lifestyle, my job consumed me. Nothing could compete with the euphoria of closing a deal, or starting a new project.

My older brother was meant for marriage, and eventually, a family. I wasn't. I was a prick when I was a player, and I was still equally disinterested in any kind of relationship now.

However, I wouldn't mind getting laid occasionally.

After a brief hello from my assistant, I seated myself in my office that overlooked downtown Denver, almost immediately checking my schedule on the computer, and losing myself in work. I hardly noticed when my assistant brought me coffee, even though I'd told her numerous times that it wasn't part of her job.

Swinging around, I finally took a sip of the lukewarm liquid and let out a satisfied exhalation, knowing that the caffeine would soon hit my system. Not that I needed to get any more pumped up, but I was pretty addicted to my caffeine, which was my only addiction these days.

I reached into the candy dish that sat on my desk, dutifully stocked by the same assistant who fetched my coffee. Since she'd gotten to know me, every piece of hard candy in the bowl was butterscotch.

"Sugar and caffeine," I mumbled, realizing how much the little things could make me content these days.

I went back to work, losing any sense of time as I planned out what I wanted to get accomplished in the next week.

Unfortunately, I could never completely get a pair of cool, ocean-blue eyes out of my head for the rest of the day.

CHAPTER 2

Paige

hat a conceited asshole!

I tried hard not to think about my brief encounter with one of the two owners of Walker, knowing I should have been more cordial. But Sebastian Walker's charming demeanor and the way he'd looked at me had put me on the defensive almost immediately. His friendliness hadn't been comfortable. Mostly, he reminded me of every rich snob that I'd come to detest.

Spoiled.

Entitled.

Ready and able to screw any woman he wanted.

Nevertheless, I'd been sweating by the time I'd left the elevator, disconcerted by his open greeting and open smile, but repelled by the way he'd surveyed me like he was trying to decide if I was worth screwing.

I put my attention back on the file on my desk, a real estate contract that needed to be completed. I loved contracts and legal documents. There was no questioning the written word. Things were either in writing or they weren't. Everything was spelled out, the document perfectly clear on terms if it was done correctly.

It was my job to make sure the contract was perfect.

I looked at the clock, and noticed it was already nearly five pm. I'd eaten lunch in my office as I wrote the contracts that needed to be issued, being extra careful to scrutinize the verbiage. Wording was important, and I didn't want to leave Walker vulnerable while trying to give them some wiggle room in case they needed it in the future.

A giddy flutter in my belly reminded me that I was really here at Walker, ready to start my career in law. I had a plan, and I had every intention of making sure my life went according to schedule. My first objective was to get to the top of the department, and someday be Chief Council at Walker, a position that was currently held by Daniel Hurst. Mr. Hurst was a highly respected attorney, a man who would eventually be retiring in a few years. By then, I wanted to be at the top of the ladder instead of writing and reviewing contracts.

Not that I wasn't grateful for my entry-level job at Walker. Nobody had been more stunned than me when I got a job with a prestigious company like Walker Enterprises, especially considering my lack of experience.

My move from the East Coast had been uneventful, but I had to admit that I'd been anxious to start my job. My new apartment was too quiet, and I was missing my best friend, Mackenzie, like crazy. I didn't have any friends here in Denver, so the separation from Kenzie, after so many years of being together in our small apartment in Cambridge, was torture. Kenzie had taken a job in New York, so she'd left our apartment a few months before me. I'd wanted something in business law, so I'd applied for every open position I could find, somewhere away from the East Coast. I'd expected some response, but never from a company as enormous as Walker.

I waved at some of the departing attorneys that I'd met earlier as they passed my office. Even Mr. Hurst was going out the door.

Once everyone was gone, I sat in the silent office, pretty sure I was the only person left in the area.

Putting my head down, I got lost in work, not allowing myself to think about leaving. Technically, I *should* be going home. But there was nothing and no one waiting there for me. I'd actually rather be here.

"Hell, I don't even have a cat," I mumbled to myself as I looked from my notes to my computer screen, trying to make sure the wording was exactly as I wanted it.

When I printed out the final contract I'd been assigned, then shut down my computer, it was dark and after nine o'clock. My stomach growled from lack of food, but I was otherwise content. The boss would be pleased. Mr. Hurst had assumed the contracts would keep me busy for a few days. I'd finished in one day, and I was ready to move on to something else.

I left the office feeling upbeat, like I'd accomplished everything I possibly could on my first day. It was going to take long hours to work my way up in the company, but I was up to that. What else did I have to do? Upward mobility was part of my plan and next on my list of things to accomplish.

As I walked to the elevator, I cracked a small smile as I thought about how Kenzie teased me about my lack of a social life. Throughout law school, I'd had to work, and I had studied a lot. I couldn't afford to get myself off-track. Focus was the only thing that got me through the day.

In my undergrad days, I'd been a lot more social, and I had attended quite a few parties. Then, one awful day, everything had changed. By the time I entered law school, all I'd wanted was to keep control over my life. And I did.

I might not be the life of the party anymore, but it doesn't matter.

One of the elevator doors *whooshed* open, startling me into reality as I hurried toward the lift. I stopped short of entering as I saw an exhausted-looking Sebastian Walker leaning against the back wall, smirking as he saw me.

Damn! What are the chances we'd end up in the same elevator...again!

"I don't bite, Paige, unless you want me to," he said in a low baritone that slithered slowly down my spine.

Everything about Sebastian made me uncomfortable, but his low, Texas drawl had instantly been my weakness. It was obvious he was highly educated, and the sophisticated accent was different; subdued but not quite tamed.

All I wanted was to let the doors close and take the next available transport down. But I didn't. I had absolutely no reason to avoid Sebastian Walker, or so I told myself. Lifting my chin, I moved into the small space and stayed near the door, stupidly pushing on the *Lobby* button, even though it was already lit. Logically, I knew slamming the hell out of the elevator panel wouldn't make the doors close faster, or the elevator go any quicker. In fact, continuing to push for a floor that was already selected was an incredibly ignorant thing to do, but Sebastian Walker rattled me, dammit.

Finally, I stopped slamming on the lighted knob like a freak, and turned around briefly to acknowledge the only other person in the elevator. "Mr. Walker." I nodded at him.

"How was your first day?" he asked politely. "Why are you still here? Everybody in legal knocks off around five."

He seemed...different. Maybe it was because his tie was hanging loose around his neck, and his jacket was over his shoulder. His sleeves were rolled up like he'd actually been working, and he sounded more low-keyed, maybe because it was getting late.

He'd come in the same time I had this morning. Was it possible he'd had a long day? "It was good," I answered shortly. "Yours?"

I had visions of him chasing his secretary around the desk all day until he'd finally caught her and nailed her on the desk. But for some reason, the image didn't stick.

I had no doubt that Sebastian Walker was every bit the playboy he'd been branded. How could he not be? Yeah, I was pretty certain the rumors I heard about him were true since I'd learned about his behavior from more than one source.

He had a body meant for sin, tall and toned as hell, intriguing hazel eyes, and thick, sandy brown hair that tempted a woman to spear her fingers into the cropped locks to see if they felt as sensual as they looked.

Still, right now he actually looked just a little bit vulnerable and more approachable.

"Busy," he finally responded to my question. "But good. I'm making progress on our solar energy interests. So my day was productive."

I gaped at him. "I didn't know Walker was big into alternative energy."

Walker Enterprises was a major conglomerate, but I hadn't seen anything remotely resembling alternative energy in their profile.

Sebastian shrugged. "It wasn't before I joined Trace. Now that area is developing and expanding. Seeking the resources so we can do what we need to do to become a world leader in technology and development is a large part of my job right now."

"You actually work?" *Shit!* I hadn't meant to say that aloud. Even my tone of voice had been insulting—surprise mixed with a healthy dose of disbelief.

Somehow, I hadn't seen him as the type of guy who busted his ass for his company. I'd heard good things about Trace Walker, but Sebastian...not so much.

His sudden bark of laughter rang out in the small space. "Why else would I be here? I don't exactly have massive orgies in my office. It's big, but it isn't *that* big. Contrary to what some people might think, I do work hard to do the best I can for Walker. It's our family legacy. Maybe you shouldn't believe everything you hear, Paige."

What I'd *heard* is that Sebastian Walker screwed a different woman every night of the week. That he was a worthless, spoiled billionaire who traveled around the world looking for his next big party.

"I did believe it. I'm sorry." I felt kind of bad when I looked at his weary expression. It was obvious that there was a part of Sebastian Walker that I'd never heard about.

We were moving down now that the doors had closed, and I felt a little sad that I'd judged him by rumors alone. My remorse was sincere. I had judged him because he was rich, was known to be a playboy, and had a bad reputation. It was hearsay, and I usually wasn't the type to judge by other people's opinions.

Maybe I had my reasons to hate wealthy, spoiled, petulant men, but I couldn't keep lumping all rich guys into the same category.

He brushed off my apology. "I did it to myself. Too many years acting like an asshole. Now I have to prove my worth here at Walker."

"You don't have to prove yourself to anyone. It's your company," I defended. "So you really haven't slept with countless women and blown off your responsibilities?"

Oh, dear God, I really, really need to muzzle myself. Sebastian Walker's personal life was none of my business, but my damn curiosity was digging me deeper into a hole. If I wasn't careful, my unusual bluntness could lose me my new position.

He grinned. "Never said *that*. I did. I don't anymore."

I wondered if he meant he didn't still sleep with a lot of women, or if he was responding to the part about his responsibilities. But it didn't matter. His sex life was none of my business.

Shut up, Paige. Just shut the hell up!

My stomach rumbled while we were silent, a growling noise that no longer wanted to be ignored. I put my hand to my belly. "Sorry."

"Did you eat today?" Sebastian asked in a disapproving voice.

I nodded. "Lunch. But it's been awhile."

"I'm starving, too. Do you want to go grab some dinner with me?"

His charming smile was back in place, but he looked more approachable, more genuine. I wasn't sure if it was my imagination, or if he *was* really more appealing at the end of the day than he'd been this morning.

His masculine scent drifted across the confined space, and I breathed it in, loving the smell of starched linen, masculine strength, and a musky aroma I couldn't place. It was all him. *Sebastian.* His fragrance lingered in the air between us like an aphrodisiac.

Strange, but I could swear that I could smell a hint of butterscotch. Unfortunately, I loved all things butterscotch, so it made his scent even sweeter.

I only let myself absorb him for a moment before I came to my senses and reminded myself he was everything I *didn't* like.

He was rich.

He had been a player.

And he was undeniably one of the best looking men I'd ever seen.

"I can't," I refused. I was a junior attorney, a newbie in his company. I didn't need to be seen anywhere with him unless it was business. People would talk.

He was also wealthy and powerful, two things that made me nervous in a very unhealthy way.

"Why?" he asked curiously. "I'm not asking you to let me fuck you, although I certainly wouldn't refuse if you wanted that. It's just food for two hungry people."

I shuddered at his bluntness, but his husky voice conjured up some very hot visions of a passionate encounter that I couldn't get out of my head. "It's late. I need to get home." Like he was desperate to get laid? A guy like him probably had women falling at his feet. I didn't delude myself for a second that a man like him actually wanted to screw me. He could have any woman he wanted.

It occurred to me that this was a highly inappropriate conversation to be having with the big boss on my first day at the company.

The elevator stopped, and he motioned me out in front of him.

The lobby was empty except for a security guard sitting at the front reception desk. Sebastian lifted his hand in greeting, and his employee waved back with a smile.

"You don't have to get home," Sebastian stated bluntly. "You just don't want to be seen with me."

I turned and faced him. "Honestly, I don't. I'm just starting the job opportunity of a lifetime, and I don't want to mess that up. I like to keep things uncomplicated." That was putting it mildly. I generally avoided men like Sebastian, like a person avoids a communicable disease.

"What's complicated about food? You're fairly new in town, and we're hungry. I don't have many friends here myself. I pulled up roots to come here last year, but all I do is work. It's just dinner."

"How did you know I was new to the area?" I asked, wondering how he knew *anything* about me. For all he knew, I could be a local.

He grinned mischievously, an expression that was nearly irresistible. "I do own the company," he answered simply.

I panicked, wondering what else he knew. Moving across the country was my escape from my past. A new start. "What else did you find out?" I asked aloud as I fidgeted with my purse.

"I know you were a model student with nearly perfect grades—"

"Nearly?" I questioned.

"Okay, pretty damn perfect. But you did get an A- in your undergraduate work."

I was proud of my obsessive overachievement that had landed me straight A's and scholarships to struggle my way through school. "Philosophy. My professor hated me because I asked too many questions," I said defensively.

"Sometimes there are no concrete answers."

"But why think about something that doesn't have a definitive answer? I like solvable mysteries."

Sebastian laughed, and the sound made my heart skitter. He was getting to me, and I had no idea why.

"You're not that pragmatic," he answered in an amused voice.

He surprised me, probably because there was some truth to his words. At one time, I *had* been a dreamer, but that had been a long time ago, and that part of me was gone.

I went to look at my watch, a nervous habit, but something I did often to keep myself on schedule and focused. Unfortunately, my wrist was bare. Somehow, my watch had been lost while I was moving and I hadn't replaced it. Right now, it was definitely a gesture of pure discomfort.

I couldn't keep letting him dig into my life, not even about little things. We had to keep our discussion short and professional. "Any other observations, or can I go now, Mr. Walker?"

"If you were looking for the time, it's nine o'clock. Dinner?" he asked, his tone cajoling.

"No," I answered huskily. Not only was Sebastian Walker an uncomfortable man to be with, but his eyes seemed to be probing me like he was trying to figure me out.

I'd made it a habit to keep everything, every emotion well concealed. He'd never understand me. Sometimes I didn't even comprehend some of my personality since I'd done such an abrupt change.

The last thing I wanted to talk about was me or my past. I wanted to look toward my future.

"The only thing I saw was your résumé and your references," he admitted. "I don't know any of your deep, dark secrets, and I don't really want to right now. What I want is to get something to eat. With you."

I swallowed hard as I finally looked him directly in the eyes. For a brief moment, our gazes met in understanding. Somehow he knew that I was uncomfortable with him, and he was trying to ease my fears. But I wasn't scared of *him*. Not exactly. I wasn't afraid for my physical safety. But maybe I *was* wary of the way I reacted to him. My body was tense, and a deep-seated need seemed to make me want to be closer to him, while my reason pushed me away.

Sebastian was handsome, but it wasn't just his looks that made me want to spend more time with him. Maybe he was just as much a mystery to me as I was to him, but there was *something* there as we continued to lock eyes and stare at each other.

He's lonely.

Just the thought of a billionaire as hot as Sebastian needing company almost made me want to laugh at the errant thought. But the thought rang true about my suspicion. And I had a feeling he understood me, too.

In the end, even though I yearned to go with him, my rational side won out, just like it always did.

"Goodnight, Mr. Walker," I said in a shaky voice as I turned and averted my eyes from his mesmerizing expression.

"I won't stop trying, Paige," he warned as I turned to exit the building.

When I'd left through the sliding doors, I whispered to myself, "I won't stop saying no." It was more of a vow than a statement.

That brief connection, the chemistry between us *had* to be ignored.

I had big goals, and I wasn't going to let my apparent lust for Sebastian Walker stop me after I'd worked so hard for the last several years. My physical reaction to him was surprising, but I admitted to myself it *did* exist. I just couldn't make it that important.

I shuddered as I entered the parking garage, almost certain somebody was watching me.

Turning, I looked over my shoulder as I walked faster, then slowing my pace as I saw Sebastian watching me as I hurried to my vehicle.

CHAPTER 3

Paige

"Oh, for God's sake, Paige, if he's that hot, just have a fling with him," Kenzie grumbled as we talked on the phone at the end of my first week at Walker. I'd told her everything. I'd met up with Sebastian a few more times during the last five days, but I'd made an effort to be completely professional. As usual, he just grinned like he knew something I didn't, and it was totally unnerving. Did he realize that my body reacted to him every time I saw him?

"I can't just screw him, Kenzie. He and Trace own the whole damn company." My best friend didn't understand why I couldn't just scratch my itch, even if I'd have to have an awkward relationship with Sebastian once I did.

Not to mention the fact that I'd never *had* a one-night stand. Not intentionally, anyway. I'd gone out with a couple of guys in law school, but the sex had been uncomfortable rather than pleasurable. The two relationships had both ended after the first sexual encounter.

Kenzie's suggestion was oddly tempting. Generally, I avoided entanglements all together. I definitely didn't want a *relationship*.

But I did have an itch that needed to be scratched. It was interfering with my concentration occasionally. Unfortunately, I had a feeling there was only one man who could soothe that discomfort, and he was absolutely off-limits.

"Then casual sex, Paige. Lord knows you're due for a fling."

Seeing as I'd never had one before, I'd say I was more like...*overdue.*

I kicked off my low heels, and flopped on the couch in my apartment while keeping a solid grasp on my phone. "Not with him."

"It's a big city. There has to be somebody."

There wasn't.

I was alone, and except for Sebastian Walker, no man seemed to see me as a female. Most of the other attorneys in the office were married, but they treated me kindly. The few females on staff in legal were older, but I liked all of them. I'd even made casual friends at work. But other than that, there wasn't a single guy I'd encountered who even tempted me to have a casual fling.

Just him.

Only Sebastian.

Dammit!

"There's nobody else," I groaned into the phone.

"Then use the hot billionaire. You said he was a player. Certainly he'd do you if you hinted that you wanted to go that direction."

He might, and that very thought terrified and bewildered me. He'd asked me two more times to have a meal with him, only to be refused. "I'm not so sure all of the rumors about him are true," I admitted to Kenzie reluctantly. "All I see him do is work late."

"Then maybe he needs to get laid, too," Kenzie suggested. "Sounds like a perfect situation to me."

"I don't *need* sex," I denied, knowing my statement was true. I'd survived years without it.

"But you *want* it," Kenzie stated. "Paige, is your reluctance because of your past?" Her voice changed to one of hushed empathy.

"No. Not really. I just don't want to do anything to jeopardize my position. I'm starting all over in Colorado. And I need this job."

"Unfortunately, you can't run away from your past when you change locations," Kenzie answered with regret in her tone.

I knew that Kenzie understood me and accepted me the way nobody else did. She had her own issues that had affected the way she sometimes saw herself, an incident that had forever altered her life. Maybe that's why we were so tightly bonded. Both of us had experienced something that had irrevocably changed our lives completely.

"I know," I admitted wistfully, wishing that my new surroundings *would* suddenly change my personality. But it hadn't. I was still the same cautious, nerdy female, determined to climb the ladder, even if it killed me.

I suddenly felt tired and wiped out emotionally, so exhausted from trying to contain every emotion.

Logically, I knew becoming as successful as possible was a control issue, or maybe just a safer place to be. But having some kind of security was important to me. More critical than giving into baser needs that I knew damn well I could live without.

"Just do him," Kenzie said with a sigh.

I twirled a long strand of my dark hair as I retorted, "You wouldn't do it. How's *your* social life these days?" Kenzie was creative, but she wasn't exactly daring. Like me, she'd once been carefree, and eager to find her next party or opportunity to socialize. Her future had been bright and ripe with opportunity.

Then one day, everything had changed for her, too.

"It sucks," she admitted. "I'm living in the big city now, but I do everything alone. Not that I'm complaining. New York has endless things to see. But nobody notices me. Nobody looks at me as a potential date."

My heart ached for Kenzie's situation. If someone could just look inside her heart for an instant, they'd see how beautiful she really was. "Truce?" I said softly. "Don't badger me about my social life, and I won't mention yours. There's nothing wrong with being alone. Not for me. I prefer it that way."

"No, you don't. You just *think* it *has* to be that way. We're both fucked up," Kenzie replied in a melancholy tone.

Honestly, we probably were both more than slightly dysfunctional because of our pasts, but I wasn't going to admit it. "No, we aren't. We're working on our careers."

"Maybe you are. Mine is pretty much stagnant."

"No chance of working your way up the ranks?" I questioned.

"Not without more education."

Kenzie had taken a job at a prestigious art gallery in New York as a receptionist. She'd been hoping she could learn and advance. Obviously, she wasn't going to get that opportunity. Even though we'd lived in a college town, my best friend had never gotten the opportunity to attend any of those colleges full-time to get a degree. She'd taken some art classes, but had worked two jobs just to survive.

"Do you need anything," I asked anxiously. New York was expensive. "I can send you money. I'm working now."

"Not happening," Kenzie answered decisively. "I have a second job at a convenience store. And I have a couple of roommates. I'll survive just fine."

God, I hated the fact that Kenzie wasn't going to have a chance to advance. After what she'd been through, she deserved to be happy. And despite the fact that she hadn't gone to college, she was smarter and definitely more creative than most people I knew who had a higher education. "Let me know. I'm working full-time now, and I have a good job."

Even as I offered, I knew Kenzie's pride would never let her accept my help. She never had.

"You also have a fortune in student loans to pay. Tell you what...you could help me by having a fling with the hot billionaire so I can live vicariously through your experience," Kenzie said teasingly.

I rose from the sofa with a chuckle. "I don't screw and tell."

"You'll spill everything," Kenzie challenged.

Normally, I *would* tell my best friend nearly everything. I always had. But then, I'd never exactly had an active, exciting sex life. "Not happening," I reminded her. "He's much too dangerous."

Kenzie sucked in an audible breath. "Did he threaten you?"

"No!" I quickly reassured her. "Not *that* kind of dangerous. He's..." Hell, I didn't know how to explain.

"He's the kind of guy who might get to more than just your body?" Kenzie concluded. "You like him."

I walked to the kitchen of my apartment, looking for food. "I don't know if saying that I like him is really appropriate. He makes me uncomfortable in some non-physical way. He's annoying, arrogant, assuming, and he has a reputation with the women. But he works hard, and I haven't really seen him with beautiful women on his arm. In fact, I haven't seen him with a woman at all. He actually works too much."

"Yep. You like him," Kenzie said with a laugh. "If he gets to more than just your body, you think it's dangerous. One sign of any emotional attachment, and you're walking away."

I opened my mouth to deny her claim, but then I closed it again. Kenzie was actually right. "I can't help it," I replied as I opened the refrigerator door. "I can't afford to get involved with a Walker."

"Wait a minute. He's not related to that crazy, reclusive billionaire that lives on an island all by himself, is he? Dane Walker?" Kenzie sounded excited.

"He is," I affirmed as I looked at the sad offerings in the fridge and closed the door. "They're brothers."

I knew most everything public about the Walker family. I'd made it a point to do my research once I'd gotten the job at Walker Enterprises. Dane Walker was the youngest, a recluse who did live on a remote island.

"Holy shit!" Kenzie exclaimed. "Dane Walker is pretty much a mystery in the art world. He studied under one of the greatest artists of our time, and then started producing his own stuff. We have a painting of his in our gallery. His work commands a hell of a lot of money, and it's hard to come by. All I know is that he's extremely reclusive and filthy rich." She paused before adding, "And his paintings touch me. He might be crazy, but he's one hell of an artist.

I was aware of most of those facts. They were public knowledge. What I didn't know was exactly why Dane Walker hid from the world. "He was injured in a plane crash when he was eighteen. His father and stepmother died. Dane was the only survivor. Maybe he was so traumatized that he wanted solitude," I guessed, really having no clue what the actual story might be.

"He's amazingly talented," Kenzie mused. "But there has to be something seriously wrong with a guy who hates civilization."

"Not really," I said defensively. Sometimes I think I'd be more than happy to get away from crowded cities. Maybe living alone on an island *would* get old after a while, but right now it sounded like heaven. "Not everybody loves living in the city like you do. There's too many people, too much crime, too much noise. I can think of a number of reasons why somebody would choose to be alone."

My chest ached as I thought about how lonely I felt sometimes, even though I was usually surrounded by people. That was who I was now...a woman always on the outside looking in, but never really participating in the world around me except in business.

"You don't have to be alone, Paige," Kenzie murmured sympathetically. "You're beautiful, smart, and now you're incredibly successful. Relax a little."

I snorted. "I'm not beautiful, and I'm not successful. Not yet. And If I'm smart, I'll keep my eye on my goals." I perched on the arm of the sofa for a moment, knowing I was going to have to go to the supermarket. "I'm only in the lower ranks. I'm just starting." Now was not the time for me to start slacking. I had too far to climb.

"Because of your life schedule?" Kenzie questioned.

"Yes. There's nothing wrong with having goals and striving to meet them in a certain amount of time. It keeps me motivated."

"It keeps you so exhausted that you can't even think about anything else," Kenzie answered drily. "Screw the schedule. You can cut loose a little. I've heard Colorado is a beautiful state. Have you seen any of it?"

"No," I answered honestly. In truth, I hadn't been outside the city of Denver. I'd had no reason to since it had everything I needed in the metro area.

"No mountain drives? No sightseeing at all," Kenzie pried, her voice astonished.

"No time."

"You have the weekends off. Go somewhere," she demanded. "I've heard the hot springs are incredible, and the mountains are awe inspiring."

"It's cold," I argued stupidly.

"And the hot springs are hot," Kenzie countered wistfully. "Can you imagine lounging in the warm water when you're surrounded by snow in the mountains?"

My mind was blank. "No." I couldn't remember the last time I'd stopped, even for an instant, to admire something beautiful. My brain was laser-focused on meeting my goals.

"Do it," Kenzie suggested emphatically. "Then call me on Monday and let me know how it was."

"I'll think about it," I said, knowing damn well I'd end up doing laundry and grocery shopping. If I had time, I might catch a movie on Netflix.

More than likely, I'd spend any free time at the office, looking over the contracts I'd been given to complete next week so I could get a jump on my workload. Now that my boss was realizing how quickly I could work, he was dropping more and more contract work on my desk. Mr. Hurst was starting to trust me, which was a good thing. But the extra workload was getting much more challenging.

"Call me Monday and tell me everything," Kenzie said in a warning voice. "And no work."

"We'll see. What are you doing over the weekend?"

"Working at my extra job," she admitted.

I rolled my eyes. "And you're telling *me* to stop working?"

"It's an easy job. My mind wanders, and I think about all of the places I'd rather be," she answered nonchalantly.

"I wish you'd come visit. We could check out all of the places you want to go," I answered, trying to swallow the lump in my throat.

Kenzie hadn't had an easy life, but her concern was always for other people.

"I'm working on it," she answered cheerfully. "In the meantime, preview everything for me."

I chuckled, then we chatted for a little while longer before we hung up, leaving the apartment completely silent.

Making my way into the bedroom, I stripped and pulled a pair of jeans and a sweater from my closet, knowing I had to either shop or starve.

Not that I couldn't live for a while since I was far from thin. That was exactly what kept me from looking at myself in the full length mirror as I shimmied into my jeans and yanked a violet-colored sweater over my head.

I didn't like the way I looked when I was naked, and I avoided checking myself out as much as possible.

I brushed out my hair and added a little bit of lipstick, not really caring what I looked like just to go shop for food.

My mother was Italian, and I'd inherited her love for carbohydrates, as well as her curvy figure. On my parent, voluptuous was a good look. My mom was tall, so she could pull off her full figure well. I was shorter than the average woman, and my lack of height just made me look...rounder.

"I'm not buying pasta today," I said to myself firmly as I yanked on a pair of boots. Denver didn't really have any snow that had stuck to the ground yet, but it was chilly.

I grabbed my jacket and purse as I headed for the door, determined to buy the items I needed for a healthier diet. I'd gained my freshman fifteen, and then some, when I'd started college. It was well past time for the weight to come back off.

I gasped in surprise as I yanked open the door, ready to dart out into the hallway, but unfortunately, there was a very large problem in front of me that I'd have to deal with before I went anywhere.

CHAPTER 4

Sebastian

I hated the fact that I was starting to feel like a damn stalker! I'd driven by Paige's apartment building three times, but I still hadn't been able to make myself go home.

Finally, I'd given up trying to ditch my idea and just parked my car and hauled my ass up to her door.

Now, as I surveyed the look of surprise and horror on her face, I was rethinking my decision. Maybe I should have found her phone number and called her *before* showing up on her doorstep. But I knew if I didn't try to persuade her in person, she might just hang up the phone.

The fact that Paige was dressed so casually and her thick, beautiful hair was down around her shoulders stopped me in my tracks. And, of course, my unruly dick noticed the more carefree look immediately.

No matter how much I loved her prim and proper office look, I realized that I much preferred her this way, her hair unbound, jeans hugging her body, and a pretty purple sweater completing her casual attire.

I knew damn well I shouldn't be here at her apartment. I'd had to go through the human resources records to even find her address. But I couldn't bring myself to give a shit if I was being a little bit unethical.

I didn't.

All I thought about lately was Paige, and every time I saw her, I wanted her more.

It didn't matter that she casually blew me off, or that she hurriedly escaped every time we ended up in the same area. She felt the same way I did, and we had a chemistry that refused to be denied. I could sense it. But for some reason, she was trying to ignore it.

"Paige." I nodded my head, not able to say much more than her name.

She looked at me suspiciously. "Why are you here? How did you even find out where I lived?"

"I have a problem," I answered hoarsely. Well, it was the truth. My dick wouldn't stop standing at attention, and it was all her fault.

"What?" She crossed her arms, still clinging to her jacket and purse.

"Can we talk?"

She hesitated, and I started to feel like a jerk. It was her weekend, her time off. Still, I wondered where in the hell she was going.

Did she have a date? For some reason, that didn't sit very well with me.

She finally stepped back and waved me inside, closing the door behind me.

"What's wrong? I finished everything ahead of schedule today," she asked, her tone now sounding concerned.

Shit. Now she was fretting about her job. That was the last thing I'd intended. "It's not anything like that. I'm not complaining about your work. I need…a favor."

I wasn't the least bit surprised when her expression changed from one of concern to a look of disappointment. God, I hated *that*.

"Is this personal? You still haven't told me how you knew my address. It isn't appropriate for you to be looking up my address at Walker for personal reasons," she admonished.

I had to hold back a snort of laughter. Only Paige would have the guts to point out that my behavior was a little unethical. "It's work related."

She lifted a dark eyebrow, waiting for my explanation. Hell, no woman could make a guy feel as shitty as Paige did when she gave me *that look*.

Finally, I just decided to spill it, and see if she'd help me out. "I have to go up to the mountains tomorrow night. I was invited to a private party to celebrate the opening of the ski season, and the gala is being thrown by a guy I've been trying to acquire a property from for months. A very rich man from the East Coast who has a vacation home here in the mountains. He's repeatedly turned down my offers. He has an abundance of real estate, but I really need a large piece of property he owns in New Mexico."

"Maybe he just doesn't want to sell," Paige suggested.

"He does. He just doesn't want to see reason on the price. I think he knows I want to develop the area, and he wants top dollar and more. I thought if I could meet with him in person, he might agree to my offer."

"You mean if he's in a party mood," Paige replied.

"Maybe," I admitted.

"You want me to do a contract so you can see if he'll sign it in person?" Paige sounded confused.

"No. I want you to go as my date. If I'm at the party with somebody, I'll have more freedom to try to get the seller alone. I have a feeling I was invited because he has two daughters. The last thing I want is to offend him. I need a buffer, a reason why I'm not interested in hooking up with anybody."

"Otherwise, you think you'll have women crawling all over you? Even this man's daughters?"

"I know so," I answered unhappily. "I can't go to a party alone without being swamped with hopeful women. I'm too young and too rich to get away with walking into a party unnoticed."

Maybe I sounded arrogant, but it was simply the truth. I didn't want to spend the whole evening making polite conversation with every unmarried female at the gala. If I was honest, I'd also admit that it was a good reason to spend time with Paige. But I wasn't going to search my damn soul to figure out why I wanted to be with her, so I decided being *that* honest with myself was completely unnecessary.

"I get that," Paige agreed reluctantly. "But there is any number of women who'd be happy to go with you—"

"No, there isn't," I interrupted. "I don't know any women here in Denver well enough to explain why I'm attending. I haven't dated since I gave up my party days. You're my only hope. I told you I work a lot, and I haven't met anyone here." It was the truth. The only woman who had caught my attention was Paige. I'd noticed her like she'd grabbed me by the nuts and never let go.

"I'm sorry. I don't do parties," she answered, opening the door to let me out.

"I'll pay you for the weekend. Strictly business." I tried to sound persuasive.

Her face was pensive as she answered, "Seriously, I'm not a social butterfly. I wouldn't have a clue how to talk to the rich and elite. I don't even own appropriate clothing. I understand your situation, but you'll have to find somebody else. Believe me, any single woman at Walker would go with you in a heartbeat."

"I want to keep it strictly business." I ignored the open door. "I'll pay you a ten-thousand-dollar bonus to go with me. And I'll pay for your dress."

I watched her eyes grow wide as she chewed on her bottom lip like she always did when she was thinking. Looking around her apartment, I noticed that her stuff looked secondhand, and the furnishings were sparse. She was a newly minted attorney, and if she went to Harvard, she was probably broke until she started earning a regular paycheck. Even if she went to the ivy league college on some scholarships, she'd still had expenses, and probably plenty of student loans.

Paige closed the door and looked up at me earnestly, an expression so torn that I almost told her to forget about it. I didn't want her that stressed out over a damn party. What I told her was absolutely true, but I *could* go alone. I just didn't want to, and it seemed like the perfect opportunity to spend time alone with her.

"You think this deal is really important to Walker?" she asked hesitantly.

"Yes. It's also important to me. It's an enormous property in an appropriate area for the biggest solar farm in the country, and a research facility," I answered honestly. I actually had coveted this property for months. It would be a perfect location, but I had to get a better price than what the seller was offering.

"It isn't that I don't want to help Walker, and I'm grateful to the company for taking a chance on me with no experience," she told me hesitantly. "If you think this will help the company, I'd go, even without the bonus. But I really do hate parties."

I could understand that. I didn't exactly enjoy rubbing shoulders with the social elite most of the time myself anymore. "Why?"

She shrugged. "Not my thing. I'm socially awkward, and I'd have nothing in common with those people."

Paige tried to sound nonchalant, but I wasn't buying her excuse. I'd seen a very real flash of fear in her beautiful blue eyes that had only lasted for an instant, but it had been there. "I'll help you, Paige. I promise."

I'd be guarding her like a Doberman now that I knew she'd be uncomfortable.

"I know I'll eventually have to learn to do useless events because of my profession," she admitted. "If I want to climb the corporate ladder, I have to learn to socialize, I suppose."

I nodded. "We do a lot of corporate fundraising events for charities, and we have plenty of charity galas for Walker."

"I'll do it," she agreed firmly. "But it has to stay business only, and I don't want the money. I'm earning a paycheck now."

"You have to get paid or it's not business," I remarked casually, wanting her to accept the payment to make her life easier.

Paige shook her head. "I make a good salary. An occasional weekend will be expected."

I crossed my arms stubbornly. "This is a favor to me. It's not anywhere near part of your job."

"If it makes Walker more money, it's job security."

I chuckled because I couldn't help myself. "I don't think we're going under anytime soon." Walker was thriving, even without the new alternative energy investments I was adding.

"I'm going to need you to help me pick out a dress. I have no idea what to wear."

I drank in the sight of her casually dressed, her gorgeous hair cascading down her back. Hell, I wouldn't mind if she went in a pair of jeans and a colorful sweater. She looked breathtaking. But I knew she'd feel out of place if she wasn't dressed appropriately. "Where were you headed?"

"The grocery store. My cupboards are bare."

Mine weren't exactly stocked, either. I'd never bothered to hire anyone to cook or shop because I was rarely at home. "I'll go with you. Since you keep refusing to eat with me, I need to stock up. We can look at dresses on the way."

Right on cue, her stomach growled, and she put a hand over it with a sheepish grin. "Sorry. I skipped lunch."

"Tonight, I'm feeding you," I grumbled. I was going to get her some dinner, whether she wanted that or not.

"I—"

"Don't argue," I insisted.

"I was just going to say that I'm starving. Can we eat first?"

I smiled as I took her jacket and held it out for her to slip into. "Food first," I agreed readily. Hell, I'd probably agree to almost anything since I was finally getting Paige to spend time with me.

Maybe it was still a mystery why I was so attracted to her, but I wasn't going to fight it anymore. I was the kind of guy who liked to solve enigmas and puzzles. Usually, I liked to tackle problems that needed an answer, but I couldn't exactly say Paige was a *problem*. But the challenge of figuring her out was just as exhilarating.

I inhaled her tempting, light, floral scent that had always lured me to get closer to her. As I gently lifted the silky mass of hair out of her jacket, I smiled broader when I realized that the cock-hardening aroma had to be her shampoo when the fragrance became just a little bit stronger as her hair sprung free. Jesus, I was sporting wood just from the smell of her fucking hair? It took every bit of control I had not to bury my face in the dark locks, pin her ass against the wall and nail her until I was sane again.

"Thanks," she murmured, taking over the job of flipping the hair from under her jacket as she moved away. "Don't you have a jacket?"

"In the car," I answered huskily, still not over my urge to let my caveman instincts take over control and nail her right there against her apartment wall.

I opened the door and stepped out of the apartment, letting her lock up. Problem was, I wanted more from Paige than just a fuck. For some reason, she intrigued me, and if I wanted to spend time figuring her out, I'd have to be patient. Funny, but I'd never really had the desire to get to know a woman all that well. Most of my adult life had been filled with endless parties, and I realized I'd never met a woman who really wanted to get to know me, either.

I fucked.

I drank.

I got high.

And I tried to forget that my dad had died much too soon, and my younger brother was scarred emotionally and physically for life.

Now my obsession was my company, which was probably a much healthier occupation than being a full-time player, and a hell of a lot more fun. But being with Trace, living in the real world where most people actually had to work hard to get ahead, I had to face the fact that I'd been an asshole almost all of my adult life. It wasn't an easy thing to admit.

"You okay?" Paige asked hesitantly as we rode the elevator down to the first floor.

I pulled myself from my own thoughts. "Yeah. Why?"

"You look so serious," she observed.

"And you think that's unusual for me?" I asked, the question coming out slightly defensive.

She frowned. "I didn't say that."

"But you think that," I grumbled.

"Actually, I don't believe everything people say. We all do different things for different reasons. You work hard now, and that's all that matters. You're obviously brilliant, smart enough to start this new division at Walker."

"Believe me, I *was* everything people talk about. I was rarely sober, and more often than not, I was as high as a kite. I moved from one party to another without a single damn thought about my brothers or what they were going through. I'd say that made me a pretty selfish man. Mostly, I avoided Trace because I knew he'd give me a lecture about growing up."

"Then why did you finally grow up?"

Really, I wasn't sure how to answer that question. "I don't know."

"Yes, you do," she argued.

"Trace, Dane, and I were all together last Christmas. I guess I finally realized what I'd given up to stay in a useless atmosphere with no real family or friends." It had been a sobering moment when I finally admitted that I hated my life. "After the accident that killed my dad and was nearly fatal for my younger brother, I ran away like a coward. I wasn't there for Trace or Dane."

"Everybody handles grief differently. You were young," Paige ventured.

"No excuses. It was a selfish thing to do. Trace could have used my help. He was young, too. And Dane definitely needed someone to be around for him."

"Did he? Did he really? I read that he lives on a private island. That doesn't sound like a guy who really wants company."

"I could have tried." There was truth to what Paige was saying. Dane *had* wanted solitude, and he'd found it. To this day, he didn't talk much about the accident that had nearly taken his life.

Paige was quiet as she followed me out to my car. I disarmed the security system and unlocked the door, holding it open to let her get in before I closed her door and settled myself in the driver's seat.

"What kind of billionaire drives an SUV?" she teased.

I put on my seatbelt and started the engine. "The kind of guy who moves from Texas to Colorado. And it's not *just* an SUV. It's a Porsche turbo with five-hundred and seventy horse power."

"Impressive," she answered sarcastically. "I guess I just never pictured you as an SUV kind of guy."

"Because I'm a rich asshole?" *Okay. Yeah.* I was a little disgruntled because she still seemed to see me as a frivolous dick.

"No. Not because of that at all. You just seem to be the type of man who likes to go fast."

I wasn't sure if it was a compliment or not, but I decided to take it as one. "Zero to sixty in under four seconds, even if it is a crossover."

I looked at her and shot her a cocky grin.

She smiled back at me before she said, "Don't let your past define you. I think we all have regrets for things we've done."

"Even you?"

"Especially me," she admitted quietly.

I wanted to ask her more, find out what in the hell she could have ever done that she regretted. For a woman her age, she seemed to have everything figured out. Yeah, it was evident that she was hiding herself from the world. But she was hyper-focused on her career, and pretty damn accomplished. I wanted to ask her what she meant, but when I saw the closed expression on her face, I decided not to push.

"Okay. Time to show you how fast this SUV can go," I decided.

I gunned the engine as I pulled out of the parking lot. When I hit the freeway, I proved my point by showing her just how quickly the vehicle could hit the speed limit.

I expected her to lecture me about being more cautious, but in those moments, I learned that Paige really *did* have an adventurous side.

She didn't ask me to slow down.

She didn't act afraid.

She didn't say anything coherent at all.

In fact, my chest ached just a little as we sped toward one of my favorite restaurants because Paige Rutledge did something I'd never heard her do.

She let out a squeal of delighted laughter that I knew would stay with me for a very long time.

CHAPTER 5

Paige

T *his was a gigantic mistake!*
          That negative thought had run over and over again
          in my mind all day. And now, as I was looking back at
myself in the full-length mirror on my closet door, I was doubting
my judgment even more.

What in the hell was I doing in a burgundy-colored cocktail dress that made me look like I belonged in a world I had no
business entering? Certainly, someday I might be required to
attend a few charity functions for Walker if I was able to fight
my way up the corporate ladder, but I was still far from being
on their guest list.

Fidgeting with one of the lacy sleeves on the over-the-top
dress I was wearing, I shuddered as I recalled the price of the
gown. Sebastian had hauled me into one of the priciest stores in
the city to choose appropriate evening wear, and I'd hastily tried
on the first few that caught my eye.

Unfortunately, they'd also been the costliest, a fact I hadn't
noticed until we headed to the check-out.

I turned around with a critical glance, admitting that I looked presentable. Hell, how could I not be? The dress was exquisite, with intricate details that would lure any unsuspecting female to try it on. It had certainly drawn me to it when I'd been looking around for something that caught my eye in the store. The cocktail length was perfect, and the silky material brushed lovingly against my calves as I moved. The top was more fitted, with intricate lace and silver beads adorning my shoulders and arms. I'd slipped on the elegant, silver heels to get the full picture.

"I can do this. I can do this," I murmured to myself, straightening my shoulders as I surveyed the upswept style of my annoying hair, held firmly in place with silver clips.

I'd done a complete makeup job, something I never bothered to do. Usually, I was brutal about pulling back my slippery, straight hair so it would hold for the day, and I did very light makeup—if I did any at all. While I was in law school, messing with cosmetics and primping was a waste of valuable study time. I'd threatened to chop off my hair to make things easier about a thousand times, but Kenzie had always talked me out of it, telling me how gorgeous my silky straight hair was, and how it would be a shame to whack it all off.

Now, I wished I had one of those sleek, short styles so I'd look a little more sophisticated and worldly.

Unfortunately, I was forced to work with what I had.

I closed the closet door, tired of wishing I could be something I wasn't. When had that happened?

I was focused.

I was driven.

I wasn't caught up in vanity to look more appealing.

"Sebastian," I said to myself with a sigh.

The truth was…I didn't want to disappoint him, or have anybody doubt that I could be a woman he was romantically interested in. I'd started out agreeing to this farce because I wanted to be loyal to my employer. But I also needed to admit that I wanted Sebastian Walker to get the deal he was working so hard to arrange. That particular wish was more personal than business.

I couldn't help but notice how hard he worked, and how much he longed to leave his old life behind. He wanted to prove himself, and I could relate to all of those things. Maybe that was why I felt so drawn to him sometimes, and why every once in a while, I was pretty damn tempted to take him up on his offer to have dinner together.

Luckily, I'd never crumbled during one of those weak moments when I felt we actually had something in common.

But I couldn't say I hadn't been tempted.

Spending time with him the night before had been danger-ously fun, but I could rationalize that as business. I was simply helping him out because Walker needed to acquire this property. But really, I knew deep inside that I wanted to help Sebastian follow his dream.

He was intelligent, and his passion for alternative energy made me admire him as a person. From what he'd said last night, the money meant very little to him. His concern was more about the future of the planet.

I scooped up my clutch purse as I made my way into the small living room of my apartment carefully, reminding myself it had been years since I'd worn heels quite as high as the pair Sebastian had insisted I buy to match my dress.

I'd drawn the line at buying a new jacket or jewelry. It was too personal, and I'd probably never wear the gorgeous dress again.

I perched on the edge of the couch to put on my great grand-mother's earrings, a gift from my mother on my eighteenth birth-day. Her mother had given them to her daughter when she'd become an adult, and my mom had followed the same tradition. They weren't expensive, but the vintage sterling silver chandelier design dangled elegantly, and it was the nicest pair I owned. To me, the earrings were priceless because they'd been in my family for four generations now.

My chest ached as I put on the second earring after brushing my finger over it lightly, having a melancholy moment as I grieved for the relationship I'd had with my parents when my mom had gifted me the set.

Since the catastrophic event that had changed my life in my last year of undergraduate work, I hadn't spoken to either one of my parents. Every year, there was a Christmas card. Every birthday brought a similar card. But other than that, we hadn't communicated.

It's been over five years.

My chest tightened, my separation from my parents almost unbearable for a brief moment as I remembered how much I missed them, even after the years that had passed.

It still hurts so damn much, almost as much as it had when we'd first parted ways.

Putting a hand over my heart, I tried to calm my rapid, staccato breathing, something I hadn't even been aware of a few moments ago as I'd let myself get caught up in memories.

"Stop! You're a grown adult. You made the decision because you felt you had to," I reminded myself angrily, forcing myself to recall the reason why my parents and I were estranged.

I couldn't and wouldn't look back now.

The doorbell jerked me out of my reflections, and I took a couple of final deep breaths to calm myself before walking to the door and opening it for Sebastian.

I guess there are a few moments in life where words simply can't be formed—and I knew I was experiencing one of those rare times when I was rendered speechless.

Sebastian was casually leaning against the doorframe, his right hand in the pocket of his tuxedo pants, looking like he owned the whole damn world and everything in it. It wasn't arrogance; it was simply his virile, confident demeanor. He didn't have a sandy lock of hair out of place, and he was breathtakingly gorgeous in a black tux. Obviously, he was comfortable in the attire, and it showed in his confident stance and the relaxed grin he was sporting as his eyes moved slowly over me, doing a double take as he scrutinized my appearance again.

"Jesus, Paige," he finally said huskily as he straightened and walked through the open door. "You look absolutely stunning."

I rolled my eyes at him. Maybe there *was* still a little bit of playboy left inside the man in front of me. "You have to say that. I'm the only date you've got."

After closing the door, I hurried over to get my best wool coat off the sofa.

"You're the only one I want," he answered in a sexy baritone that almost made me believe him. Almost…but not quite.

Nevertheless, I felt a spark of heat slither down my spine and then land squarely between my thighs as I sensed his eyes were still watching me. My body always reacted to Sebastian, while my rational mind wanted to run away as warning bells screeched through my brain. I suppose the complete opposite reactions of my brain and my body weren't really all that strange.

Sebastian was hot. Probably the most agonizingly handsome guy I'd ever seen. I'm pretty sure any female would have to be married or dead not to notice him. However, I was a woman who had learned to let my brain figure out what was good for me, and it was definitely on high alert every time I saw him.

My treacherous body had a totally different response.

"This is business, remember?" I tried not to react to his musky, masculine scent that still contained a tantalizing hint of butterscotch as he helped me into my jacket.

Usually, I'd probably flip off any guy who did the old-fashioned things that Sebastian did. My womanhood would probably be annoyed if a man thought I was so helpless that I couldn't open my own car door, or put my jacket on by myself.

Surprisingly, it didn't bother me at all. Sebastian did it so effortlessly and subconsciously that it was difficult to take offense. Good manners had obviously been taught to him at a young age, and I wasn't even sure he was aware that he was being politely old fashioned. Or maybe this was just the way things were done in his world. Either way, it was actually kind of...pleasant. The gestures felt more respectful than chauvinistic.

"Screw business for just a minute, will you?" he replied gruffly. "Give a guy a minute to appreciate a beautiful woman."

Finally, I turned around and saw the heated look in his eyes, surprised by the very real expression of a man who finds a woman attractive. "I'm not beautiful. My freshman fifteen was actually an undergrad twenty that I never did manage to lose. My lips are a little too big for my face, and my nose is too small. My hair is so straight and fine that I can't do much to fix it. My breasts are barely average, and my ass is too big." Really, those last two things were probably the most important.

"Bullshit!" Sebastian's expression changed to one of displeasure. "You're fucking perfect. If you weren't, my dick wouldn't be so hard it's almost painful every time I see you. And what the hell kind of fragrance do you use in your hair anyway? It's like a damn aphrodisiac."

I stared at him in complete confusion. "I use shampoo."

"Cock-hardening shampoo," he shot back accusingly.

A startled laugh escaped my lips as I realized he was serious. "It's just...shampoo. It smells like cherry blossoms." I'd bought the wrong brand by accident right before I'd started working at Walker, and I liked the way it moisturized my hair, so I'd just used it rather than wasting it.

I covered my mouth to hide my delighted smile, but another giggle escaped as I saw his affronted expression. "I promise you, it's not intentional," I told him jokingly. "It's grocery store shampoo, and you're the only man who has found me that attractive in a very long time."

"Because you're hiding," Sebastian answered. "For some reason, you don't want to be noticed, you don't want to be discovered, and you definitely don't want to draw a guy's attention."

I sobered at his insightful comment because it contained a grain of truth. "Maybe I don't," I replied evasively. "Can we go now and get this over with?"

I was done talking about my issues.

He reached into his pocket and pulled out an envelope. "Your payment."

I shook my head. "I told you I don't want it. I meant it."

"Then it's not business," he answered huskily.

I took the paper from his hand and tore it into small pieces before stepping into the kitchen to toss it in the trash. "It's still business," I warned him as I stopped in front of him.

He grinned. "Nope. Now that makes you my real date."

He actually sounded happy about that fact, and it was confusing as hell. "No. But you do owe me a favor now," I answered lightly.

"Name it," he shot back immediately.

I'd been joking, but he was dead serious. "I was kidding. I'm doing this for Walker and for you. I know how much this project means to you." Maybe I was also going to this party for myself, but I wasn't ready to admit it. "Besides, I did promise my best friend I'd get out this weekend. But I'm not quite sure this is exactly what she wanted."

"What did she want you to do?" Sebastian asked curiously.

"She mentioned the hot springs and the mountains. So at least I'm making it into the Rockies."

"It's dark. You won't see a damn thing. If I'd known you hadn't seen anything, we could have left early."

I frowned. "In this dress? I'm not exactly dressed for exploring. Besides, she doesn't have to know it was dark. It's beautiful country, right?"

"Amazing," he agreed. "We'll go during the day sometime," he promised.

"Thanks, but I doubt we'll be out together again." Somehow, that actually saddened me.

He hesitated for an instant, looking like he wanted to say something, but then nodded toward the door. "Let's go."

Desperate to change the subject and lighten the mood, I asked, "Why is this rich guy celebrating the ski season? We're only into November." It was chilly, but there wasn't any snow on the ground in Denver.

He answered as I locked the door. "There is plenty of snow at higher elevations, and they make additional snow if they need it."

I put the keys in my clutch. "Are we going to a high elevation area?"

"Yes."

"I haven't gotten much outside of Denver yet. Do they have a hot spring there?" I wondered if the place was a resort.

Sebastian held out his arm politely, and I automatically curled my hand around it.

"Not at this resort. But there are plenty of places to go where there are hot springs," he mused. "My cousins own a resort where you can find one everywhere." He hesitated for moment before adding, "Well, I guess they aren't exactly my cousins, but cousins by marriage. My cousin Gabe married Chloe. But I've spent some time down in that area looking for property, so I've hung out with all of them. They feel like blood family. Chloe's mom insists I call her my aunt, even though she technically isn't. It's actually kind of nice since we don't have a lot of the Walker family left. It's a big family, and they've pretty much adopted me and Trace into the fold. Unfortunately, they've never met Dane."

"The Colters," I murmured quietly.

"You do your homework," Sebastian answered with some levity.

"Blake Colter is one of my senators now. Of course I know who they are and that they're related to you by marriage. I researched Walker extensively when I knew I was going to work there, and I tried to get as much info as I could about living in Colorado."

"I think a person either likes the mountains or they don't," Sebastian observed.

"Do you like it?" I asked curiously.

"Actually, yeah. I do." He paused before asking, "Do you?"

I shrugged. "Pretty much all I do is work."

Sebastian settled me into his vehicle before he admitted, "Me, too. But I've been around in search of property, so at least I get around some. Your friend is right. You need to get out, Paige."

His deep voice was far from casual. It was almost as if he knew me, understood me better than I comprehended myself sometimes. I glanced up and our eyes locked. It *was* already dark, but Sebastian had parked directly under a streetlight.

It was one more of those moments when I couldn't speak, but a silent communication flowed between us that was almost frightening. It was a familiarity that seemed so strange between two people who hardly knew each other.

He lifted a brow in challenge, and I knew he was talking about so much more than just going out and having fun.

"I can't," I whispered longingly, caught briefly in a spell that I couldn't escape.

"You will," he rasped. "When you're ready."

The connection was lost as he finally closed the car door. I shook my head, trying to understand what had just happened. It wasn't possible that Sebastian really understood me, right? It was just some kind of freaky thing that just…happened.

I shook my head as he got into the vehicle and started it up, not-so-successfully trying to convince myself that none of the brief moments when I felt my strange pull toward Sebastian had ever really happened.

He was hot.

He was smart and a fun companion.

So far, he'd been polite.

But he absolutely *did not* fill some kind of perceived emptiness inside me.

Essentially, we were strangers, and I reminded myself of that repeatedly throughout the long trip into the mountains.

CHAPTER 6

Paige

I sipped my second glass of champagne carefully, watching Sebastian as he attempted to make his way toward the opposite end of the swanky country club where the party was in full swing.

We had yet to see the man hosting this lavish event, but after Sebastian had heard his target was on the other side of the venue, I'd told him to go find him.

He'd wanted me to accompany him, but I knew he needed to get this rich owner alone, and I'd been here long enough to lose most of my apprehension. Really, my fear of going to a party had been mostly in my head, a barrier I'd just needed to break through.

I watched from a quiet corner of the elaborate ballroom, noticing that Sebastian hadn't gotten very far.

Even though he'd never left my side as we ate expensive appetizers and had a drink together, staying close to make it fairly obvious that we were together, women were all over him the moment he'd stepped away for a few minutes.

God, it annoyed me that the women were so damn obvious, shoving their surgically enhanced boobs into Sebastian's face like that would instantly make him take notice. Maybe that worked for some guys. But I could tell he was on a mission right now, and trying to be polite when he was actually annoyed.

Funny that I could sense his mood. There was a fake, polite smile on his face, but I could feel his impatience, even though there were quite a few yards between us.

I know because I've seen his genuine, mischievous grin. It was so much different than what I was seeing right now.

"For God's sake, leave him alone," I mumbled aloud, getting a little bit irritated myself.

For some reason, I didn't like watching women drape themselves all over my date. Okay. Maybe it wasn't *really* a date, but those women didn't know that.

Even if some of them had spent a fortune on plastic surgery, every one of the females surrounding him were beautiful socialites, dripping in gems, and wearing gowns that made what I was wearing look like a bargain basement special. The gowns that adorned their annoyingly perfect bodies were obviously custom, and probably cost more than I made in a year right now.

I squinted, trying to figure out if the sparkly gems on their dresses were actually real. God, that would be a horrible waste of our natural resources.

A small, secret smile formed on my lips right before I took another sip from my glass, remembering what Sebastian had said about my shampoo. Really, it *had* been pretty funny. It was an inexpensive brand, but he'd looked damned serious about the fact that it got him hard.

Still, he was deluded if he thought I could compete in looks to any of those women who had the money and time to shop, go to the spa every week, and probably starved themselves or worked out all day to stay thin.

I wasn't jealous...well...except for the fact that they were all over my date. There was a certain satisfaction in working for everything I wanted, propelling myself upward to have a better life. I had brains, which I told myself was much better than having large breasts and a tiny waistline.

I frowned as I let my mind wrestle with the problem of getting Sebastian to where he needed to be.

"Right," I said as I finally came to a decision. "I'll take care of it."

I threw back the rest of the alcohol in my glass and set it on the crisp white linen on one of the numerous tables around the room.

I plowed through the people between me and Sebastian as carefully as possible until we were face-to-face. I carefully peeled off every female hand adorning his body, boldly wrapped my arms around his neck, and pulled his head down. "Kiss me," I whispered into his ear.

I'd already learned that Sebastian wasn't a man to miss an opportunity. His arms came around my waist so quickly that I could hardly acknowledge the tight hold before his mouth swooped down on mine.

I absently registered the fact that he certainly wasn't shy about public displays of affection. I was too busy absorbing the hard feel of his body and the large, warm caress of his hand as he cradled the back of my bare neck, his mouth demanding everything he wanted, anything I was willing to give. A frantic desire I'd never experienced before bolted through my entire body, and I felt like every nerve ending I had was frenzied as I speared my fingers into his hair, relishing the feel of him almost literally devouring me.

I moaned against his lips because I couldn't stop myself, pushing my body against him, wishing I could crawl inside Sebastian and never leave.

When he finally lifted his head, his eyes were dark and mesmerizing, leaving me without a single doubt that he'd been as affected by the embrace as I had been.

"Be careful what you ask for, Paige," he drawled quietly next to my ear before nipping the sensitive lobe. "You might get more than you bargained for."

I expected him to release me. A quick glance around told me the women had left. But he moved forward, forcing me to step back. My back hit the wall, and he shielded me from curious glances even as he pinned me into a small corner.

"I was trying to create a diversion," I answered, my voice little more than a squeak.

"Oh, *I'm* definitely diverted," he answered huskily as he kissed me again.

I didn't have time to tell him that I was trying to help him get rid of the female pests. My body was already responding, my core clenching with need as he thoroughly conquered my mouth before leaving a hot trail down my neck with his tongue.

My hands fisted in his short, coarse locks, and I was using every ounce of control I had not to let out a throaty moan of desire.

I was only partially successful.

"Sebastian. Stop. The women are gone," I said, feeling a low growl from his chest vibrate against my sensitive breasts.

"I don't want to let go," he argued, nipping at my bottom lip before soothing it with his tongue.

"You have to. We're making a scene." I didn't want to lose this intimate connection with him, either, but I knew we either had to stop, or we'd end up banging each other against the wall. "I'm not into being watched," I panted as I pushed weakly against his chest.

"Shit!" He stepped back reluctantly, his eyes still smoldering with heat. "I've wanted to fuck you since the minute I saw you in the elevator for the first time. It's hard. Literally."

As he gave me space, he still shielded me from prying eyes. "Do you think those women are convinced that you aren't taking them home tonight?"

"I never planned on taking them anywhere," Sebastian replied irritably.

"I know. I could tell."

"The only woman I want to take home with me is you."

My heart skittered as I realized he was telling the truth. "I can't," I whispered regretfully.

"Can't or won't?"

I smoothed down my dress nervously. "You're in the clear. Go get your deal."

He lifted a questioning brow. "You're never going to convince me that you only kissed me to complete this mission."

Honestly, that was how it had started out. But all of my good intentions had been blown to hell the moment he touched me. "It *was* my motive."

"Until it turned into something else," he shot back. "I'll probably have that sexy moan in my mind for a very long time."

I actually flushed. Because...yeah...I had been into him, so far gone that I hadn't been able to stay in control. "Are you going to go find your target or not?" I didn't want to talk about that kiss anymore. It left me feeling vulnerable, and I hated that.

The fact was, I had lost sight of my original intentions because Sebastian made me crazy.

Not.

Good.

I was generally focused, but he had made me lose sight of my objectives. I'd wanted him so badly I'd wanted to crawl up his muscular body and beg him to put me out of my aroused misery.

"I think you should come with me," Sebastian said as he reached out and pulled me to his side.

His muscular arm curled around my waist, and he ran a teasing hand down my hip as he propelled me forward with him, toward the other side of the room.

"Quit with the wandering hand," I demanded in a furious whisper as I reluctantly let him keep me at his side.

I'd never really wanted to get this close during our deception. My reasons were originally to help out Walker, and Sebastian.

Act like his date.

Then step aside as he charmed the stubborn property owner.

Pretty simple, right? Why was everything suddenly becoming so complicated?

His stroking hand stopped, his grip now firmly on my waist.

"Damn shampoo," he grumbled, leaning closer even as he complained.

I couldn't help but deliberately look down at his crotch, but his tuxedo jacket was closed, and very little was revealed. "You look fine," I observed as we skirted the crowd by staying close to the wall.

"You think so?" he rasped, then suddenly grasped my free hand and turned me into him, making sure my palm landed directly on his fly.

I copped a feel, just because I was surprised by how hard and erect he felt. And so damn good. The jacket might be hiding his aroused state, but my fingers could feel the truth.

And Jesus, he was big.

He jerked my hand back so it was no longer between us and asked gruffly, "Convinced?"

We moved on, but my body was tingling from the feel of Sebastian's hard cock. I was a rational female, and I'd just experienced tactile proof of something he'd been trying to tell me all night.

I actually do turn him on.

Shamelessly, I looked up at him with a delighted smile. "Yes. It was kind of *hard* not to notice."

Okay. It was a corny joke, but some secret part of me loved the way his body reacted to me.

"Very cute," Sebastian mumbled in a low, disgruntled voice.

"I thought so," I remarked with satisfaction.

I had the feeling that it was rare that Sebastian Walker didn't get exactly what he wanted.

"I see him," he replied, changing the subject.

Untangling myself from him, I stayed with my back against the wall. "Then go do what you came here to accomplish."

He strode forward with an I'll-argue-with-you-later-and-I-intend-to-win warning glance before he strode to a table where an older gentleman was seated with a few other men that I knew Sebastian would probably intimidate out of the picture very shortly.

One of the guys rose after a few minutes, obviously excusing himself, and walking off into the crowd. Not long after that, the second male stood up, and turned around as he finished off his drink and sat it on the table.

It was the first time I had seen his face because his back had been to me.

He was young.

He was blond and handsome if one didn't know him—but I recognized him almost immediately.

I didn't need to be close enough to see his eyes. I already knew they were gray, cold, and calculating when he wasn't laying on the false charm.

"Oh, my God," I whispered in panic, knowing that he'd spotted me. "No."

My heart started to race and I began to gasp for air.

Following my fight-or-flight instinct as I moved into a full-blown panic attack, I turned and pushed my way into the crowd, trying to put distance between me and a man who had shaped my life in ways I never could have imagined.

He caught my wrist as I passed the bar, turning me around to face him.

"Hello, Paige," he said in a smooth baritone. "Fancy meeting you here in Colorado."

I yanked on my wrist, frantic to get away from him.

"Let me go, Justin," I said in a tremulous voice.

"You know I never let a woman say no to me," he reminded me with a malicious smile.

Bastard!

I hated myself for feeling a very real fear as he studied me carefully. "Let me go or I'll make a scene," I threatened, even as my body trembled.

"I'd prefer to get you a drink," he countered. "You look amazing. The years have only made you even more attractive."

I shuddered with revulsion. "Fine," I agreed weakly. "I'll take a drink."

I'd die before I'd take anything he offered, but as I'd hoped, it forced him to let go of my arm long enough to flee.

I ran like I was running for my life, memories that I'd closed the door on long ago bursting into my mind as I ducked and weaved until I hit the exit and flew through the door that led outside.

Panicked, I hadn't even thought about the snow and ice I'd have to navigate in insanely high heels. Instantly, I slipped and tumbled down the marbled, cement steps, not even noticing the pain as my knees and palms connected with the sharp ice and cement.

I scrambled to my feet as quickly as I'd fallen.

Desperate, I headed onto a lawn with calf high snow, hoping nobody would follow since it was dark once I left the entrance area and stepped off the treacherous sidewalk.

My mind was focused on only one thing.

Escape!

Run, Paige, run.

Finally, I stumbled into a small wooded area, oblivious to the tree branches hitting my face as I clawed my way into what I hoped was safety.

Exhausted, unable to go any further, I landed on my hands and knees in the snow.

Please don't let him follow me.

Tears started to flow down my face, and I could hear the harshness of my breathing. One sob escaped my lips, and then another as I relived the event that had changed my life.

The fear.

The humiliation.

But the thing I'd hated most was the helplessness.

"Paige?"

The male voice sounded behind me, and I couldn't help the terrified scream that left my mouth and rang out in the previously silent darkness.

CHAPTER 7

Sebastian

I'd sensed her fear.

Even across the space that separated us, I could feel her tension and watched her body language as she'd quickly escaped the spot where I'd left her.

I'd finally had my chance to speak to Mr. Talmage alone, and I'd simply blown it, excusing myself only moments after Paige had left.

After catching a flash of her burgundy dress as she'd fled through the door, all I'd had to do was follow her crazy path of footprints through the pristine snow to find her.

What the hell?

Hearing her strangled sobs had been like taking a dagger in the chest, and her ear-piercing scream of terror had me dropping into the snow beside her and trying to protect her icy-cold body from the elements.

She struggled, trying to claw at my face as I subdued her by pinning her hands over her head and covering her with my body. "Paige. Stop. It's me. Sebastian. I'm not going to hurt you."

I couldn't see her clearly in the moonlight, but I felt all the fight leave her as she started to realize who I was.

"Sebastian?" she choked out on another sob.

"It's me." I stood and lifted her out of the snow, confused, but I didn't really care why she was crying or scared. My only instinct was to protect her from whatever had upset her.

She'd dropped her small bag by the sidewalk, and I dropped it on top of her body to get a better grip as I trudged back through the snow, my feet almost numb with cold as I headed back to the building.

"No. Please. I can't go back. I can't do this. I'm sorry," she said in a terrified whisper.

"Then we won't go back." I'd be damned if I'd take her somewhere that was only going to increase her fear. "I'll take you home."

Changing direction, I headed toward the parking lot. "Are you okay?" Maybe it was a stupid question. Paige obviously *wasn't* okay, and she definitely *wasn't* the type of woman to freak out over much of anything.

In the light of the parking lot, she shook her head and clung to me with her arms around my neck, her face buried in my chest. *Goddamn it! What in the hell had happened?*

I was damn near running as I arrived at my vehicle, needing to find out whether she was sick or injured. I'd hardly seen any emotion from her other than her determination to succeed.

Now, she was literally falling apart.

I opened the passenger door of my SUV and settled her in the seat. "Are you sick? Hurt?"

She shook her head, a blank expression on her face now. I could see scratches on her cheeks and forehead, probably from colliding with the bushes and trees I'd found her in. Her lace sleeves were torn, her elbows abraded, and on further inspection, her palms were in the same state. "You are hurt," I said angrily.

"I fell. Can we please go. I'm okay."

Christ! She sounded so sad and frightened that I raced around to the driver's side and started up the engine, hoping the heat would kick in quickly and we'd both thaw out.

Since the location seemed to be part of her issues right now, I got us on the road and headed back down the mountain.

She was shivering, and I glanced over at her as she wrapped her arms protectively around her body.

We were both silent as I navigated the highway. The drive back to Denver would take a while.

Finally, the heat started blasting, and I could feel my wet pants and saturated shoes and socks beginning to warm up again.

"You have to tell me what happened, Paige. Do you need to go to the hospital?"

"No. Please. I don't want that."

"Then tell me," I insisted.

"I'm so sorry. You didn't get your talk with the seller, did you?"

"Fuck Talmage!" The last thing on my mind was a lost opportunity. I was too damn afraid to care whether I lost a hundred deals. All I wanted was to have Paige back again.

"Talmage?" she asked hesitantly.

It was too damn dark to see her eyes, but I didn't need to. I could hear the trepidation in her voice. "Ervin Talmage. The seller."

"Oh, God. He's Justin's father."

"Yeah. I met Ervin's son when I got to the table. Cocky bastard," I remarked, still confused. "Do you know Justin?"

"Yes," she replied, her voice devoid of emotion now. "I didn't realize it was a Talmage function."

"Old boyfriend?" I asked, hoping to God she'd say no. I didn't want to picture Paige with another guy.

"I met him right when I was graduating with my bachelor's degree," Paige confirmed.

It didn't escape my notice that she hadn't really answered my question.

"Did you date him?" Okay. Shit. I *was* annoyed.

She let out a humorless laugh. "You could say that. Things didn't go well. I kind of had a meltdown from seeing him after all these years."

There was something more to her story. "You still care about him?"

She was silent for a moment before she responded. "I hate Justin Talmage more than I've ever hated anyone."

"Must have been a pretty bad breakup," I guessed.

"It was. Horrifying, actually."

"Tell me," I urged, wanting to know exactly what had happened.

She sighed, sounding resigned. "We met in my last month of school before I was supposed to continue on to Harvard Law. He can be charming when he wants something. We had a class together. Occasionally, I'd help him out with some of the course-work for finals. It wasn't a difficult class, but Justin was a spoiled, rich guy, and he wasn't used to working to finish anything."

I was quiet, hoping she'd continue.

"He asked me out a few times, but I turned him down at first," she admitted.

"I know how that feels," I rumbled. She'd turned me down enough times for me to relate.

"Don't ever compare yourself to someone like Justin. He's...evil."

I felt both elated and relieved that she didn't find me to be equally as vile as Justin, but I feared that this story wasn't going to end well. "How did you end up going out?"

"There was a party for graduation. I didn't have anybody to go with and he asked me to ride with him. I was honest and told him I didn't want anything but friendship with him, but I'd ride along with him since I didn't have a car."

"You actually went to college parties?"

"During my undergrad years, I was a different person. I studied hard, but I liked to have fun. I went to a lot of parties. I was…a lot more social. He changed me that night."

I'd had a tiny glimpse of her fun side the first time she'd rode with me in my car. She had loved the power and the speed. Hell, she'd even laughed, a sound that still rang in my head at the oddest of times. Unfortunately, I'd never heard the sound again, and I wished that I could figure out how to make her that happy more often.

"So you ended up changing your mind and dating him?" Damned if I didn't see red every time I thought of Talmage touching her.

"No. It was the last time I ever saw him."

"Why?"

"He was an asshole," she stated evasively.

"Did he hit on other women?"

"No."

"Then what did he do to make you this upset?"

"He wanted more than I wanted to give," she said shakily.

"Unrequited love?"

"He didn't love me. He just wanted to fuck me," she answered angrily.

I gripped the steering wheel hard, angry that Justin Talmage had badgered her for sex. The desire was either there or it wasn't. If Paige had made herself clear that she wasn't interested, it must have made her uncomfortable to have him trying to score. "Tell me what he did," I growled.

"We went to the party, and I have to admit I did have one drink. He moved on me, but I kept having to tell him no."

I maneuvered from the mountain highway to the freeway, able to increase my speed since the freeways were fairly clear. "I'm guessing he didn't want to accept the fact that you didn't want to be with him?"

Hell, I was relieved she hadn't slept with Justin. Still, I wondered why she'd been so upset over seeing him again. Sure, it would be awkward between them, but her reaction was a little too over-the-top for there not to be more to her story.

"Did anything else happen?" I asked, knowing for Paige to actually hate someone, Talmage must have done something pretty shitty.

"Yes. That's why I hate him. He turned my whole life upside down, changed me irrevocably. I try not to think about it, and I thought I'd finally succeeded. Seeing him again just brought back memories of one of the worst periods in my life. I'm sorry I freaked."

"It doesn't matter."

"But you probably missed your chance at the property."

"Fuck the property, Paige. What in the hell did Talmage do to make you hate him so much?"

"You'll probably find it unbelievable," she warned.

"I won't. Just tell me why you dislike him, why he can throw a woman as strong as you into a panic."

She took a deep breath before continuing in a hushed voice. "He knew he couldn't get me drunk enough to have sex with him. I'd told him my limits before we got there. I partied, but I knew where to draw the line, even back then. I only had one drink, and I never even finished it."

I waited patiently because I knew there was more, and if I spoke, I was afraid she wouldn't spill the answer to the question I needed to hear.

Paige was hyperventilating again as she continued, "When he realized I was not going to give him what he wanted, he took matters into his own hands."

Instantly, I knew what she was going to say, and I felt like I'd been sucker punched. I was holding my breath, hoping to God she wasn't going to utter the words I definitely didn't want to hear.

But she did.

"He raped me," she admitted in little more than a whisper, confirming my suspicions, and my greatest fear.

CHAPTER 8

Paige

*H*e *raped me.*

I hated saying those words, and worse yet, I didn't want to go back to one of the worst periods of my life now that I was trying to move on. However, seeing Justin again, after all the years that had passed, catapulted me back to a time I just desperately needed to forget.

Tears rolled down my cheeks in the darkness of Sebastian's vehicle, and I was glad he couldn't see me clearly. I hadn't been this big of a wreck in years. My hands were shaking, my heart was racing, and as I let my head slam back against the headrest, I think I just gave up trying to avoid telling Sebastian the whole truth.

I knew I had looked like a lunatic when I'd fled into the snow, and now I sounded like I was losing my mind. How could I explain away what happened?

I couldn't.

Jumbled visions kept coursing through my brain about *that night.*

The helplessness.

The fear.

The complete humiliation that I suffered after Justin had simply taken what he wanted. Hell, I hadn't even been able to put up much of a fight.

"Why isn't he in jail?" Sebastian questioned angrily.

"I never pressed charges against him," I admitted, the rage I'd felt back then coming back to me as I remembered that my rapist had gotten away with repeatedly violating my body as I laid there naked and unable to fight back.

"Why?"

"I went to the party with him willingly. He brought me a drink. He slipped me a roofie or some kind of mind-altering drug. It took over my body so fast that everybody just thought I was drunk. It wasn't difficult for him to get me away from the crowd and into an empty room," I told him shakily, swiping at the tears that were still trickling down my face.

"A date rape drug? Where you conscious?"

"Yes. But I was so dizzy, and I felt like I was in a dream state. Sometimes I felt like my mind was outside my body, but I also had periods where I was lucid and I knew what he was doing. I couldn't stop him. I couldn't fight. I couldn't even call for help." My voice was cracking under the tension and anxiety of reliving the experience. "And I was scared."

God, it felt good to admit to somebody that I'd been terrified. During the moments where my mind could process what was happening, I'd wondered if Justin had planned on letting me live to tell the story of what was happening at the time.

Sebastian's tires squealed as he braked hard and maneuvered off an exit that was pretty much deserted. He parked in an empty lot of a grocery store.

Before I could process what he was thinking, he had his seat back and was hauling me into his lap.

I went willingly. For once, I accepted the comfort and safety he offered.

"I don't like hearing that you were scared," he grumbled as his strong, muscular arms tightened around my body. "I wish I'd known. I would have killed the bastard. Tell me the rest."

I buried my face in his chest and wrapped my arms firmly around his neck. I was shivering uncontrollably, even though the vehicle was still running and warm. "I lost track of time, but I know he raped me more than once. When he got bored, he finally took me back to my apartment. I passed out on the trip home. Some of the details are still blurry, but I woke up naked in my bed the next morning." I knew I'd never forget my confusion, and then terror as I started remembering parts of the night before. I still didn't have a lot of clarity about the whole incident. I just knew what had happened.

Sebastian started a gentle rocking motion, like he was comforting a child. I should be horrified, but I wasn't. It was the only time I'd felt safe when I was alone with a guy in years.

The sobs I'd been holding back started to rack my body, and I let myself pour everything out. There was no stopping it now.

The pain.

The anger.

The fear.

The helplessness that I'd hated the most.

"You're okay, Paige. I promise you that he'll never get near you again," Sebastian crooned softly.

Rationally, I knew no one could protect me, but for just a moment, I wanted to pretend his words were true. I wanted to believe that being cocooned in his arms would always keep me from harm. "I hate him. I hate him so damn much," I choked out painfully.

"I know, baby," he rasped. "Me, too. I wish you would have gone to the police."

I took a few deep breaths to try to calm down. "I wanted to. But my father worked at Talmage headquarters in New Hampshire, only an hour away from where I was going to school.

I didn't want to let Justin get away with what he did, but my parents begged me not to come forward in public when I told them. My dad worked in the accounting department of Talmage Corporation, and Mr. Talmage was the CEO. The Talmage family is well-known and respected in New Hampshire. They finally convinced me not to go against a family that powerful. Who would believe me? Justin was their golden child, their only male heir. I had no proof. By the time I told my parents, the drug was through my system. I don't think all of the drunk people at the party thought anything unusual happened."

"Was your father afraid of losing his job?"

I swallowed hard, trying to get rid of the lump that suddenly formed in my throat. "I'm sure he was," I hedged.

That incident was the sole reason for my distance with both my parents. For so long, I'd resented them for not supporting me. I'd wanted to go to the police. My mom and dad talked me out of it, literally begging me not to do it. In the end, I'd done what they advised. Honestly, my impression was that my dad hadn't wanted to lose his job, even though he was far from being an executive.

Money had come before his daughter's violation. It had been a tough pill to swallow for me, but I'd accepted it.

"You've never seen Justin after that night?"

"No. We were graduated, and I had gotten accepted at Harvard. I cleaned the stuff out of my share of the apartment and left for Massachusetts a few days later."

"No way was that bastard going to an ivy league school, even if he was rich," Sebastian observed gruffly.

"He didn't have the grades. He was going back to live with his father."

"I'm so sorry, sweetheart," Sebastian said as he nuzzled the side of my face in a gesture meant to comfort. "No woman should ever have to go through something like that."

"He literally just used my body when I was in no position to fight," I answered, furious all over again from just thinking about Justin's violation. "The drink he'd brought was going to be my one and only glass of alcohol that night. I had a lot to do before I left New Hampshire, and even though I was social, I also studied a lot."

"I know. That's obvious by your grades. They were perfect."

"They had to be. I also needed an off-the-charts LSAT score, and I got one. It was extraordinary enough to get me admission to Harvard."

His fingers stroked over my hair rhythmically, his hands and body constantly comforting me, although I was pretty sure he was doing it unconsciously. I'd never taken Sebastian for a cuddly type of guy, but right now, he was surprising me by how capable of those actions he really could be.

He let out a masculine sigh. "You know I can't just let this go, Paige. He needs to pay for what he did."

I shook my head. "No. It's over. Even now, I couldn't take on a Talmage. And I have no proof."

"Non-legally then. I don't give a shit how he hurts. I just want it to happen. It fucking kills me to imagine you going through that with practically no support," he snarled.

"None," I admitted. "I didn't tell anybody except my parents. I finally told my friend and roommate, Kenzie, a year or two after it happened. You're the only other person I've told. After my parents convinced me not to move forward and press charges, I kept it to myself."

"Why me?" Sebastian asked huskily.

"Because I blew your deal. Because I turned into a crazy woman. Because I went there to accomplish something for Walker and failed." Damn! I hated that.

"You didn't fail," he replied forcefully. "Jesus, Paige, I never would have gotten you anywhere near any Talmage if I'd known."

"I know. But this probably blew your chances of a deal."

"Fuck. The. Property. There are plenty of other places to make a deal. Do you really think I'd have anything to do with any

Talmage after what you told me? He could offer me the price I wanted, but I'd turn it down. I can't do business with a man when I want to kill his son," he replied empathetically.

My throat tightened, and tears sprang back into my eyes. How long had it been since someone other than Kenzie was willing to take my word about what had happened that night? How long had it been since anyone would even care? Knowing Sebastian was willing to blow off a prosperous business deal just because of what had happened to me touched me like nothing else could.

However, I wasn't willing to let him go to prison for assaulting Justin. He was talking in the heat of the moment. I knew Sebastian wasn't a murderer. "You can't kill him. They'd put you in jail," I said reasonably, even though I was once again blubbering like an idiot.

"I can't let this go," Sebastian replied, his voice vibrating with emotion. "The bastard needs to pay."

I reached up and stroked his face. "Just knowing that you believe me is enough."

His arms tightened around me. "Hell no, it's not enough. Some piece of shit violated you, Paige, drugged you and took your power while he was doing it. How in the hell do you forget something like that when he was never prosecuted and put in jail?"

"I had to. I would have lost the case. I can see that more clearly now than I did before I went to law school. And my dad would have lost his income."

"Jesus Christ! This makes me bat-shit crazy! No wonder you fucking hate rich men."

I could hear the anger and frustration in his voice. "Don't, Sebastian. I lived with it. I even thought I'd been able to forget it until tonight."

"You've never forgotten it. You just hide your pain better than most people," he argued.

I swiped the tears from my face, thinking about how strange it was that I was sitting in a dark vehicle just off the freeway, crying more than I've cried in years. Spilling my guts wasn't easy for me, but the darkness and Sebastian's concerned, comforting embrace had made it slightly easier for me to get real.

Eventually, I'd have to gain control, go back to my safe place where no one could hurt me again. But I allowed myself to wallow in a sense of security I hadn't known since before I'd been attacked.

"I'm not hiding," I protested. "I just...need to be in control."

"Because some bastard took away your choices. You feel like you have to fly under the radar, and not be noticed."

"I want to be noticed for my accomplishments," I told him indignantly.

"I doubt anyone could ignore them," he answered drily. "I'm sure your parents are proud."

I shrugged. "I wouldn't know. We don't really speak much anymore. We haven't since my parents talked me out of pressing charges."

"Did they believe you?"

"I don't really know. I was so hurt back then that I didn't ever ask that question." Was it possible that my parents had gotten me to back off because they weren't sure the incident ever happened, or was it all because my dad worked for Talmage?

The possibility that they might have thought I was too drunk that night to remember what had actually happened made me even sadder. I'd never given them any reason to doubt that I was telling the truth. I was a perfect student, a good daughter who never got into trouble, and I'd loved them both with all my heart. Probably still did, even after all of the heartache and distance between myself and my mom and dad.

"You're thinking," Sebastian mused. "Don't overthink the situation with your parents."

"I'm not," I hedged. Really, I was. Now I wondered...

"Yeah. You are. Whenever you're quiet, I know you're thinking."

He was right, which I found slightly annoying. How was it that Sebastian could read me so easily when I knew next to nothing about him? Every action had been a surprise tonight, and his immediate belief in my confession shocked the hell out of me.

Since he had a big business deal riding on having a decent conversation with Mr. Talmage in person, I'd expected questions, and possibly some skepticism.

There was absolutely none.

Finally, I answered, "Maybe I wasn't thinking about my parents."

"You were," he countered arrogantly. "I put doubt in your mind. I wish I hadn't asked if they believed you."

"It's a legitimate question."

"Were they good parents?"

"Yes. I thought they loved me as much as I loved them." My voice quivered with emotion.

"Then they believed you. They were probably trying to protect you. Maybe it wasn't what you wanted back then, but I doubt your father was as worried about his job as you think. Their daughter was raped. I can't imagine how hard that would be to accept and deal with as a parent."

Reluctantly, I untangled myself from his arms and climbed back over into my own seat before I answered. "Like I said, I wouldn't know. They didn't talk about it. They were too worried about the possibility that I'd make a police report."

Sebastian had to fasten his seat belt again. He'd apparently taken it off when he'd yanked me into his lap. I was securing my own when he asked, "Do you miss them?"

"Yes," I replied honestly.

"Losing your parents somehow makes you feel a loneliness you've never experienced before," Sebastian agreed as he maneuvered his vehicle back onto the freeway.

I knew he was speaking from experience. "I'm sorry about your mom and dad, and your brother."

"You remember everything you read?"

"Of course," I teased in a smart-ass voice, hoping we could get off the subject of my assault. "I always do my research."

"What did you find out about me when you studied Walker?" he asked curiously.

Knowing Sebastian the way I was getting to understand him now, I didn't want to answer. "Just the public knowledge stuff." My answer was meant to be vague. After his kindness, I didn't have the heart to say anything bad about him.

"You found out I was a player. That I slept with legions of women, drank all the time, and got stoned as often as possible. Maybe you saw that I didn't work, didn't care about embarrassing my family by doing some shitty things in the past."

"Yeah. The press wasn't always kind to you," I admitted quietly.

"They didn't have to be. I *was* that man. Every single word you read was true," he revealed flatly.

My heart sank. "I don't believe all of it."

"You should," he answered casually. "I doubt any of it was that embellished. I'm basically an asshole."

I frowned in the darkness, not quite sure I wanted to hear anything more.

CHAPTER 9

Paige

My curiosity about why Sebastian still identified himself as the useless player he used to be won out against other parts of my brain telling me it was none of my business.

"You're not that guy anymore," I assured him. I hesitated before asking, "How did you get so into alternative energy?"

"You want to change the subject," Sebastian accused.

"Maybe. Just answer." Really, there was nothing I wanted more than to *not* talk about what happened to me. It was too raw right now.

"I'm an engineer by education. Even during school, I messed with alternative energy. Our resources are finite, and the demand is higher than what can be provided. That means we'll eventually run out. Technology has to move ahead. The United States isn't the leader in solar right now, and we should be. Hell, someday we'll be breaking into space-based solar power and mining asteroids."

I could hear the enthusiasm in his voice. "You think we'll actually be able to do it?" I'd read about both of those possibilities.

"Probably not in my lifetime," he admitted. "But I can do what I'm able to do now."

I was fascinated by the way his mind worked. Most people only gave a damn about *their* lifetime. They didn't care what happened hundreds or thousands of years after they were dead. "I'm so sorry about the property, Sebastian," I whispered, feeling guilty after I heard how much he wanted to get more things rolling.

"Not important," he replied coarsely. "I'll find another place."

"Do you miss your old lifestyle?"

"No. It was only a way to run away from losing my dad after I graduated from college. Soon after that, I started to hate it. That's why I worked on solar development long before I came back to Walker."

I hadn't known he'd done *anything* before he'd come back to his father's company. "Then why didn't you join Trace earlier?"

"I didn't know if I wanted to. I really wasn't sure where I belonged. Trace had already moved ahead without me because I was still in school. Dane practically went into seclusion as soon as he was well enough to leave the hospital. One minute I had a family, and the next moment, they were gone," he explained.

"I know the feeling," I answered wistfully, leaning my head back against the plush leather and closing my eyes.

Once, I'd been the treasured only child of two parents. Then, suddenly, I had no one.

Sebastian continued, "When I wasn't drifting around the world for parties, I tinkered with alternative energy research at home in Texas."

"The world needs people like you, Sebastian," I told him quietly.

He was so smart, so different than any guy I'd ever met. Somehow, he'd always wanted to make a difference, contribute something valuable to society. My heart ached for him that he'd never really understood just how special he was, or how much he mattered.

"The world needs another privileged rich guy?" he answered in a self-deprecating tone.

"You work harder than most," I argued. "So what if it took you some time to find out where you belonged. You lost your dad and your stepmother, and you almost lost Dane. Trace was busy trying to take over your dad's company. It's no wonder you felt...lost."

God, did I remember how *that* felt. When I was suddenly on my own with no family to call my own, I'd felt the same confusion and loneliness. I'd just filtered mine into getting ahead so I never had to feel helpless again. Sebastian had suffered in a different way, but I understood exactly how he'd felt.

"After Justin violated you, did you feel lost?" Sebastian asked gruffly.

"Yes. Especially after I didn't have my parents anymore."

"You're not alone, Paige." His declaration was comforting and fervent. "And I swear you'll always be safe."

Yeah. Okay. I knew it was a false promise. Nobody could ever guarantee the safety of another person. But just for now, I wanted to pretend that he could. How did he know that underneath my bravado, I was always scared, afraid of being helpless and alone again?

I let myself wallow in his vow, feeling content to just let myself trust him for a brief period in time.

He reached a hand out in the darkness and captured mine, entwining our fingers together in a silent gesture of support that lulled me into a sense of security that made me sigh wearily.

I was so comfortable that I must have fallen asleep because the next thing I knew, I was awake, and Sebastian was lifting me out of his car.

"What happened?" I asked, startled as I instinctively wrapped my arms around his neck.

"We're home," he stated quietly.

I woke up quickly. "You can put me down. I must have fallen asleep."

"Be still," he warned. "Grab your purse."

He bent slightly and I scooped the clutch from the passenger seat. "I'm awake now."

"I noticed," he answered, sounding amused. "You stopped snoring."

"I don't snore," I answered, affronted.

"Maybe not. But you make the cutest little noises when you're sleep. Not quite a snore, but you sure breathe heavy."

I'm pretty sure if I really did snore, Kenzie would have told me. She would have seized on any opportunity to tease me about it.

I looked around, noticing we were nowhere near my apartment building. "We aren't home. Where are we?"

"My place," he answered abruptly. "You're staying here. After what happened, you need some time to sort through seeing Justin again. And I don't want you doing it alone."

"I can deal with it," I answered defensively. Really, nobody had ever coddled me or made a big deal about my emotions. Probably because I rarely showed them to anyone.

He set me carefully on my feet as we arrived at the garage door. I turned and looked behind me, noticing there was another vehicle in a second parking spot. It was a bright red sports car, but I couldn't place the make or model, probably because I knew very little about expensive cars. But this one caught my eye immediately. "What kind of car is that?" I pointed toward the sporty red vehicle.

He turned as he pushed the door open. "Vintage Ferrari. Pretty rare."

"It's beautiful," I murmured, admiring the sleek lines and the pristine appearance of the vehicle.

"It should be. It took me years to restore it. It was pretty messed up when I bought it."

"You did it yourself?"

He shrugged as he motioned me into the house. "Pretty much. I needed some consulting occasionally."

I gaped at the car, then back at him as I passed him on the way into the house. A week ago, I would have said that Sebastian Walker probably never lifted a finger to do dirty work. But somehow, the fact that he tinkered with old vehicles didn't surprise me once the knowledge sunk in completely. He was an engineer, and he was obviously fascinated with the way things worked and how he could improve them.

Strangely, the image of him greasy and sweating while he was restoring an old car didn't seem that odd at all.

"You did an amazing job. It looks like brand new."

He grinned at me as he shot past me to lead the way. "It's not supposed to look brand new. It's supposed to look new in the sixties style."

"Mission accomplished," I teased back.

"My dad liked old cars. He never restored them himself, but he had plenty that he bought and had done for him over the years."

I moved into the enormous gourmet kitchen behind him. Obviously, old cars were an interest Sebastian had gotten from his father. "Do you still have any of his?"

"No. My stepmother hated riding in them. My dad sold off his last vintage model right before he died."

I stripped off my wet heels, not wanting to damage his gorgeous wood floor. My stockings were dry, but they were a mess, the damage I'd done from running through the trees evident.

My polished toenail peeked out of one of the skin-tone nylons. "I guess this pair is ruined," I said awkwardly.

"Trash them," Sebastian suggested. "I'll find you something to wear."

They were thigh highs, and I didn't think twice about reaching behind me to lose the tattered garments. "I need to go home, Sebastian. I can't stay here."

"You're not going back to your apartment. You think too much," he grumbled as he took off his jacket and tossed it on the kitchen counter.

I struggled out of one leg and was working on the other, all while trying not to expose myself by hiking up my dress in the front. I was finding out the task wasn't all that easy. "Of course I think," I snapped back at him.

"I don't want you to remember what happened. It sucks when you start replaying things over and over in your mind."

I opened my mouth to tell him I'd do no such thing, but I knew he was right. I'd live every detail all over again. Seeing Justin had opened a door I'd kept locked in my mind for so long that I thought I'd forgotten.

I hadn't.

I'd just learned to put it away.

"I'll be okay." Staying with Sebastian was so damn tempting. When I was with him, I could forget my own name if I could just keep on looking at his big, toned body and ever-changing hazel eyes. He fascinated me. Teased me. Made me feel…safe.

Yeah, I knew it was an illusion. He was Sebastian Walker, and I was a new, entry-level attorney who shouldn't even have a reason to speak to him. Now he knew the majority of my secrets, all in the span of one evening. To be honest, it was pretty unnerving.

I'd spent years trying to shield myself from getting hurt, only to have Sebastian break through those walls in an amazingly short amount of time. Had I not run into Justin, I wouldn't be feeling so vulnerable. Sebastian would have never known the shame I hid. But now that he did, I wasn't sure where to go from here.

"Hey, you're thinking again," Sebastian teased as he dropped to one knee. "Let me do this."

My breath caught as he competently grasped the top of my second stocking and lowered it slowly down my leg. I looked at the top of his head as he bent to do a task I'd been fighting to finish for the last few minutes.

The warmth of his fingers on my bare flesh forced my body to react instantly, conjuring up visions of Sebastian stripping off my clothes for a far different reason. *Jesus!* I wanted to see this man naked and aroused more than I've ever wanted anything. The compulsion was so strong that I nearly couldn't control it.

He stood and drew the garment through his fingers, like he was having fantasies of his own.

"Are you dry?" he asked huskily as he toed off his shoes. "I think the only thing that's still damp are my shoes."

My mouth was as arid as the desert. Watching him toy with my stocking had been one of the most intimate acts I'd ever experienced, and he hadn't even been touching me.

It took me a moment to comprehend his question. I was as wet, slick, and ready as I'd ever been in my life. The only thing damp was my panties, but I couldn't tell him that. "Yeah. I-I'm...good."

My hesitation made him glance my direction and he lifted a wicked eyebrow in question. "Problem?"

"No," I reassured him hastily. "Not at all."

I was such a liar. My heart was hammering against my chest wall, and my body was clamoring to climb on top of him naked just so we could be skin-to-skin. I had a feeling I could never get close enough to Sebastian for my liking, but I sure as hell wanted to try.

Relief coursed through me as he turned and carefully laid my stocking on the kitchen counter on top of his jacket.

I have to leave. I have to get out of here.

Panic started to take hold as I realized that I couldn't be with Sebastian without yearning for something more than friendship. Don't get me wrong...I liked him. He'd been kind and compassionate tonight, and that touched my heart. But there was no way my body was going to be satisfied when I was around him without having some serious carnal knowledge of his ripped, toned body.

My worry was that it wasn't just lust. Some strange weakness drew me to Sebastian, and it wasn't something I was familiar with.

"Here. Relax and have a drink," Sebastian suggested calmly as he held out a glass of white wine, holding a tumbler of something that looked a little stronger in his other hand.

I stared at the glass of alcohol being offered to me, and I visibly flinched and shook my head desperately. "No," I entreated.

That was all it took for me to have flashbacks of another time and place, the door completely opening and the memories rushing back in a flood of horror.

CHAPTER 10

Paige

FIVE YEARS EARLIER...

I still couldn't quite believe I was on my way to Harvard. Elation flooded my soul, and I smiled and looked around the crowded room, the party rocking and the thrumming of the loud music echoed the beat of my heart. Many of these people were my classmates, all of us ready to go out and conquer the world in one way or another.

The graduation party was in full swing, and I was breathless from dancing with one of the guys from my class, all of us giddy with relief that our final semester was over. Some of my friends were moving on to master's programs.

But me...I was going to Harvard Law School.

My parents had been so proud when they'd heard that I'd gotten accepted. I was applying for scholarships and grants, but I knew that I was going to have to take student loans and work while I was attending the prestigious and expensive law school. But not even the cost of my education could dampen my spirits.

I was going to freaking Harvard, and I was sitting on top of the world right now.

Maybe I didn't need an ivy league education to help women and kids who didn't have a voice. I'd known exactly what I wanted to do since I started high school, and I knew I'd need a law degree to accomplish my goals. But it would make me a better lawyer. And the disadvantaged people in this world deserved someone who could help them be heard.

I always knew I was one of the lucky ones. I had good parents who had made me their entire world as long as I could remember. We didn't have a lot of money, but I knew I was loved. Mom and Dad had done everything they could to help me through school, and I knew they were going to be my rocks when I was in law school.

My parents had taught me that there were more important things than money. As an attorney, I'd do okay financially, but I wasn't exactly planning to be a high-powered corporate lawyer. But none of that mattered. I'd be happy. I'd have a purpose, and I could make a difference in people's lives.

It was the only thing I'd ever wanted to do.

"Here you go, Paige." The male voice drew me from my thoughts.

I reached out and took the cocktail from his hand. "Thanks."

Justin Talmage was just a friend I'd made fairly recently. I liked him, and I helped him with his classes, but there was no romantic interest between us. Well...not for me, anyway. I'd felt bad every time I'd turned him down for a date, but the feelings just weren't there. He was handsome, charming, and utterly eligible since his father was a very, very rich man. But I dreamed about meeting a guy who had my same passions, my same interests. A man who would be a best friend and a lover who would finally make me feel some of the same reactions that my girlfriends felt when they had finally discovered the right guy.

Me? I hadn't found that certain somebody yet. But I knew I would someday. Maybe it wouldn't happen until after I finished law school, or maybe I'd meet him there. It didn't bother me that he hadn't shown up yet. I was willing to wait. And my mom had told me that I'd know when the right one came along. I knew she was telling the truth. She always did.

I sipped my drink slowly, wishing I didn't feel so guilty that I couldn't seem to muster up any romantic feelings for Justin. He'd been pursuing something more since we'd become friends a few months ago. I'd hesitated when he'd offered to bring me to this party, but he'd assured me he was okay with just being friends.

"How is it?" he asked, sounding anxious.

"It's good," I assured him. "Thanks."

I wasn't sure what I was drinking, but it was sweet and tangy at the same time. I liked it...whatever it was. Not being much of a drinker, I'd asked Justin for something on the weak side. I had packing to do, and I didn't have time to be hungover.

"I have a feeling you're going to love it," he replied, smirking at me as he watched me take another swig.

I was thirsty after dancing like a crazy woman, going full-speed on one of my favorite songs. My drink was already more than half gone as I tipped the glass again, knowing I was consuming the one drink I was allowing myself tonight pretty quickly. But I didn't care. I could get a Coke after I was done.

The music was loud, and the swarm of bodies usually didn't bother me. I'd been to tons of college parties. I was used to the craziness, and I generally thrived in this atmosphere. But suddenly, I started to feel dizzy and my head was spinning.

"You okay, Paige?" Justin asked calmly.

"Yes. No. I don't know." I couldn't shake the reaction to the alcohol I'd just consumed.

Weird. I've had more than one drink, and I've never had this kind of reaction before.

Justin grasped my arm and pushed me forward as my brain became strangely disconnected from my body.

I couldn't think.

I couldn't talk.

All I could do was stumble into a vacant bedroom with Justin right behind me, his forceful hold starting to hurt my upper arm.

"You have no idea how long I've waited for this, Paige. I'm not a man who takes 'no' for an answer. Deep inside, you know that you want this."

My ability to struggle was pathetic as he yanked at the zipper of the casual dress I was wearing, jerked it over my head, then pushed me backwards until I fell onto the bed.

I blinked, trying to focus on his face as he tore off my bra and panties, vaguely realizing that I was completely naked.

His face never entirely came into focus, but I could tell he was removing his clothes. "No!" I finally choked out pathetically. "No."

His laugh was slightly maniacal. "I told you not to say 'no.' I don't like that word," he answered angrily. "I know you really want it, but I'm thinking you probably want it rough. You think I'm a nice guy and not capable of giving you what you really need?"

My very distant, rational mind knew Justin was becoming unhinged, but I couldn't bring myself to fight. My mind and body weren't coordinating.

I knew he was going to rape me, and I was helpless to stop it from happening.

Terror rose up in my mind, an ice-cold fear that left me horrified.

"No!" I tried to scream, but nothing came out of my mouth.

I felt like I was floating.

"You a virgin?" Justin asked as he crawled onto the bed naked.

I couldn't answer. My body was incapacitated, and my voice was non-existent. I became more and more confused, and a brief thought that I was somehow drugged flitted through my mind before I once again became puzzled and bewildered.

I felt the pain as Justin invaded my body, but I couldn't shout out. I couldn't even cry. There was nothing I could do except bear the humiliation of him grunting on top of me as my body stayed unresponsive.

After the first time, I didn't bother to even try to fight. My limbs were numb, and my humiliation had turned to fear that he was eventually going to get rid of me so I could never tell anybody what had happened here this night.

I fought losing consciousness, but I wasn't always successful. I went in and out as Justin completely violated my body over and over again. Each time I woke up, I'd find him ramming himself inside my body. At one point, I was face down on the bed, and Justin was fighting to jam his cock inside my ass. I was actually grateful to pass out soon after, the pain forgotten as I sunk into the darkness.

My nightmare took on a surreal quality as I woke and slept, each time rousing confused. All I wanted was for it to be over. I desperately wanted control of my body again.

Finally, I awoke without the fear of losing consciousness again. I was weak and nauseous, but I knew I wasn't in jeopardy of lapsing back into the black hole I'd been swallowed up in every time I woke.

I sat up carefully, realizing I was back in my own apartment and in my bed.

"Jesus. What happened?" I muttered, every muscle in my body screaming with pain.

It took me some time to acclimate, trying to figure out how I'd gotten so hung over. I was never much of a drinker. Had I overindulged? Had Justin brought me home?

I pushed back the covers, not entirely certain that I wasn't going to vomit.

That's when I noticed that my sheets were a bloody mess.

Underneath my ass, crimson stains littered the white sheets, and recollections flooded back to me slowly.

I wrapped my arms around my own nude body, rocking back and forth on the bed as reality hit me, and I couldn't stop remembering what had happened the night before.

It took a long time for me to get out of bed, take a shower, and get dressed, knowing the only ones I wanted to run to were my mom and dad.

Fear had engulfed me like a large cloak, and I left my apartment terrified that Justin was lying in wait.

By the time my parents arrived to pick me up, I was hysterical, jumping into the back seat of the vehicle, sobbing with relief, knowing that what had happened to me would change my life forever.

I just never realized how much.

CHAPTER 11

Paige

"Paige! Come on, sweetheart. You're scaring me."

Sebastian's voice jerked me out of my memories, and I clung to the soothing sound with a desperation I couldn't explain.

I closed my mouth when I realized I was screaming, begging for my invisible assailant to stop.

"I'm sorry," I answered, feeling horrified that I'd literally fallen back into one of the worst nights of my life. "When I saw that glass of wine—"

My entire body was trembling as I came back to the reality of the present.

"Don't," Sebastian interrupted in a graveled voice. "I understand."

"I'll take that wine now," I told him breathlessly, still trying to not relive something I'd barely made it through in the first place.

"I'll bring it and you can pour your own," he suggested, towering over me.

"No. It wasn't you, Sebastian. I guess being handed a drink was a trigger for me. Justin got my cocktail for me and drugged it. I've never accepted a drink from anybody after that happened. I order my own drinks." I didn't want Sebastian to believe that it was *him* I didn't trust. Truth was, I didn't take drinks from *anybody* because of my history.

He scowled at me for a moment, then went and fetched our drinks.

I grabbed it immediately and took a couple of gulps, still panicked and shaky from the vivid memory of the event that had changed me, changed my life.

I was desperate to relax, and for some reason, I didn't question my choice to accept the wine from Sebastian without fear this time.

He sat down next to me as he undid his tie. "Jesus! You took ten years off my life," he rasped. "Does this happen often?"

"Never," I admitted. "I had nightmares for a while soon after it happened. I went to counseling when I got to Cambridge. Things got better, but the counselor did say that I might have triggers that could set things off when I was stressed. It's never happened."

"I'd say that seeing your attacker would qualify as a stressful situation."

I sipped a little bit more wine from my glass, and I was starting to unwind from the tension that had unwillingly taken over my body and mind. Now that I was back in control, I was embarrassed by my lack of command over my emotions in front of Sebastian. "Look, this isn't your issue. I'll be fine at home."

"It *is* my issue," Sebastian growled as he set his drink down on the table. "I'm *making* it my issue."

"Why?" Now that I was more coherent, I still didn't understand why Sebastian even cared.

He took the wine from my hand and set it down on the table next to his. "I have no fucking idea," he answered, sounding frustrated. "But I promised you that you'd be safe, and contrary to what anyone thinks, I take my promises seriously. Did he chase you down at the gala? Is that why you were outside?"

I swallowed hard, my heart racing just from thinking about Justin pursuing me. "Yes. But he doesn't know where I live."

"You're connected to me because you were there with me. It wouldn't be difficult for him to find you."

"What does it matter? I'll call the police." My answer sounded braver than I felt. I struggled between my need to gain control and the fear that was still trying to swamp me when I thought about Justin being here in Colorado.

I'd left the East Coast to escape my past. Instead, it was now stalking me.

Sebastian's eyes were flashing with anger, and some other emotions I couldn't identify. "I know he hurt you, Paige. Understand that it will *never* happen again."

Oh, dear God, there it was again, that expression that I really didn't understand on Sebastian's gorgeous face. It reminded me of possessiveness, but it wasn't quite *that*. He wasn't exposing a selfish or malicious demeanor. He actually looked...worried.

I was holding onto my façade of bravery, but just barely. His stubborn need to protect me sent me over the edge. It was a new and heady feeling after being so alone for so long.

What would it feel like to be...adored and protected? Even if it *was* only my imagination that was making me feel that way.

He stood and grasped my hand. "Let me show you to your room. Don't argue with me. You'll stay here where I know you're fucking safe."

My desire to disagree was slowly fading. I was so dazed and fatigued that my spirit had very little fight left, and I knew I wouldn't sleep a wink if I was home alone.

I barely glanced at the beautiful living room we passed as he led me to an elevator to access the top floor.

"You have an elevator in your house?"

He shrugged. "Comes in handy when a lot of things need to go upstairs." He hesitated before adding drily, "I think I've grown rather fond of elevators since I met you."

I smiled weakly back at him, remembering the times we'd met in an elevator. I had to admit that it seemed pretty normal to be riding up in an elevator with Sebastian's scent driving me insane in the small, enclosed space.

I knew I was going to cave in and stay here, at least for tonight. I was weary and wrung out like a limp dishrag. Emotional overload had set in, and I wanted to be someplace safe to sleep it off. "Thank you," I uttered quietly, more grateful for his unexpected kindness than I could express.

As we exited the lift, he asked, "For what? For keeping a promise?"

"For being you," I answered honestly.

Sebastian was a conundrum I hadn't quite figured out, but he'd been so concerned and empathetic. And I was almost a stranger to him. He didn't need to accept the responsibility of protecting me after my encounter with Justin, but he seemed to take the job on his broad shoulders without a second thought.

A soft light flicked on remotely as we passed through the entry, and it revealed one of the most beautiful rooms I'd ever seen. Just the bedroom was as big as my apartment, and judging by the door on the other side of the large space, I assumed it had a connected bathroom. Decorated in an elegant coastal theme with soft blues and greens, it wasn't the kind of room decorated to intimidate or impress.

It was a space to relax.

"It's gorgeous," I said in a soft, breathy voice, still trying to take in my surroundings.

"Rest. Chill out. There's clothing in the closet. I'm not sure what's there, but help yourself. I'm going to go take a shower."

Before I could thank him again, Sebastian was gone. I heard the sound of a door closing just a short way down the hall, so I was fairly certain his room was probably next door.

My bare feet sunk into the luxurious carpet as I walked toward the closet, finding that it held more than a few articles of women's clothing. Most of the attire was casual: jeans, T-shirts, sweaters, and flannel shirts. I finally found a simple cotton night-gown, and I pulled it from the hanger, feeling guilty that I was borrowing someone else's clothing.

Before my regret actually set in, I noticed that the garment still had tags on it.

It's brand new.

I wondered if it belonged to an old girlfriend who'd never had a chance to wear it, but as I went to close the closet door, I noticed that many of the items still had tags.

"I hope whoever owns them doesn't get pissed off," I mumbled to myself, so eager to get out of the dress I was wearing that I headed toward the bathroom.

While I anticipated a hot shower, and getting out of a gown that was still a little damp along the hem, limp and cold, I was seized by a sense of anxiousness I hadn't felt in a long time.

The en suite bathroom was just as gorgeous as the bedroom. I looked longingly at the bathtub and sighed, wishing I could sink into that much hot water and try desperately to warm my soul again.

I was emotionally exhausted, scared, and feeling the old sense of shame and helplessness that I'd experienced right after Justin's rape. For years, I'd buried it, tried to focus only on my future.

Tonight, that technique just wasn't working.

I'd gone to counseling, but my old ghosts had come back to haunt me, and I hated feeling vulnerable.

I stripped off the lovely gown, mourning the fact that it was most likely beyond repair. After taking off my panties, I washed them by hand and hung them on one of the many hooks around the room.

The shower was hot, but it never did warm the cold, empty places inside me that I now seemed to notice still existed.

The bathroom had everything, and every item was new. I unwrapped a hair brush and started running it through my freshly-washed hair and donned the nightgown, looking at my reflection in the mirror.

My eyes looked…haunted, which was exactly how I felt. I hated Justin for coming in and turning my life upside down all over again. He'd turned me into a frightened rabbit, and I resented that.

Worse, Sebastian had been there to watch me crumble. I loathed Justin for that, too. Granted, Sebastian had been support-ive, and I'd be forever grateful, but no professional woman wanted to lose it in front of one of the owners of her new employer.

"Bastard!" I said fiercely as I remembered the smug expression on Justin's face tonight, using more force on my hair than was necessary to get it brushed out.

"Talking about me again?" Sebastian said from the doorway.

His voice startled me, and my body visibly jerked as I turned my head to see him leaning against the doorjamb, looking just as confident in a pair of sweatpants and a T-shirt as he had in a tuxedo.

His hair looked darker because it was still wet, and his lips were turned up in a teasing smile.

"Not you," I admitted as I yanked the brush through my hair again and faced back toward the mirror.

Looking at Sebastian was dangerous. I wanted to dive into his passionate nature and see what it was like to truly be bold.

In business, I was confident.

Personally, I was basically a recluse.

Yeah, I made the excuse that I was busy with my career. But I was actually a coward, afraid to experience life the way Sebastian had. I'd never traveled, and I'd never been free enough to do anything spontaneously. Not that I wanted to go from party to party. But I'd like to know what it was like to have some kind of fun in my life. It had been so long, I couldn't remember the last time I'd done anything without careful planning, except for the gala I'd agreed to attend with Sebastian tonight. And that spontaneous decision had turned out badly. Very badly.

He moved behind me and snatched the brush from my hair. "You'll pull every lock of that beautiful hair out of your head," he said in his lazy drawl. "What's wrong?"

Sebastian brushed my hair out carefully and gently, waiting for me to answer.

"Other than the fact that I can't seem to pull myself together, I don't know." I didn't admit weakness to anyone except Kenzie. But I was tired of lying to myself.

I *wasn't* always strong.

I *wasn't* always brave.

I *was* human.

I had basic needs that I'd pretty much ignored since I'd been violated by one of the most vile, narcissistic pricks I'd ever encountered. Yeah, I'd put on a great façade, an act that only Kenzie had ever been able to look through to see the real me.

Sebastian stood behind me and gently finished brushing my hair, seeming to actually relish the task. "You don't always need to be together," he observed gently.

"I do," I replied emphatically.

"What's going to happen if you don't? The world won't end if you take some time to recover."

"It's been years since the incident happened," I argued. "I should be over it by now."

Our eyes met in the mirror, and once again, I was overwhelmed with a feeling of connection with him. His hazel gaze actually calmed me.

"Sweetheart, some things you never quite get over. You just learn to move on and deal with the emotions when they come up," he drawled.

"I didn't think I'd ever feel like that again," I revealed shakily.

I *had* moved on, but maybe I'd never quite gotten over the unfairness of the situation. Justin had gotten away with violating me, and when I saw his face tonight, every emotion I thought I'd never feel again rose to the surface: anger, fear, regret, vulnerability, and a paralyzing helplessness, all of them stripping away the sense of safety I'd worked so hard to gain.

"You have the right to feel angry and afraid," Sebastian answered as he put the brush down and wrapped his arms around my waist from behind. "Don't keep trying to hide it, or those feelings will eventually eat you up inside."

I let my head fall back on his shoulder, grateful for his muscular, strong body and the way he seemed to sense what I was thinking.

He knew how I felt. His every soothing word eerily confirmed that for me. "Did you let your emotions eat you alive?" I asked curiously.

"Plenty of times," he admitted readily. "But there comes a time when you just face them and quit running away."

Is that what I'd been doing all these years? Had I been avoiding getting back into real life again by insulating myself with school and business? "When did you know it was time?"

He dropped a tender kiss on my cheek. "I suppose it's different for everybody. But I knew when I saw my brothers again and realized they were doing something with their lives. Hell, even after everything Dane had been through, he was creating art and making a name for himself. It made me realize how useless to society I really was, how far removed I'd become from anybody who might give a shit about me. I think I wanted to drive them away."

I thought about that for a moment before I asked, "Why?"

"Because I'd never found my own strength. I didn't actually believe I had any. When you numb yourself with booze and getting high, you don't have to really do any self-reflection. You just...float."

"Am I hiding?"

"I'd bet my life on it," Sebastian answered immediately. "I see it in you because I know that escape so well myself."

His voice was husky and rough, and I knew he was sharing a part of himself that he rarely revealed to anyone.

I wanted to be just as honest.

Turning around, I put my arms around his neck and tilted my head back to see his face. His expression was raw, his eyes exposing his every emotion to me. My heart skittered because I knew opening his tormented past wasn't easy. He was doing it for me, so I would understand he'd been where I was right now. I suddenly wished I could have been there for him when he'd struggled with his life-changing events.

Words flowed from my lips in response to the way he'd made himself vulnerable. "I used to be idealistic. Corporate law wasn't my first choice. But I thought it would make me more powerful, so I focused on whatever gave me strength. When I was an undergrad, I thought that I'd meet the right guy, and I never gave up hope—even though most of my friends already had a steady boyfriend by the end of my Bachelor's program." I sighed tremulously and drew another quick breath just to get everything out there. "My mom used to say I'd just know when the right man came along. I'd never felt that way with anybody before Justin raped me."

"Yeah, Trace told me the same thing about meeting the right person." Sebastian's expression turned suddenly grim. "What are you trying to say, Paige? Please don't tell me that—"

"Yes!" I exploded as I interrupted him. "I want to tell you. I was a virgin when Justin raped me."

CHAPTER 12

Sebastian

I'll kill that motherfucking bastard!

I'd known what Paige was going to say before the words painfully left her mouth, and a fury like I'd never felt before consumed me. Maybe I was just used to being stoned or drunk, so I'd never had particularly violent reactions to anything. But I knew it was more than that.

Thinking about Paige being innocent and completely unable to protect herself while some demented prick played with her made me completely insane.

I was trying to stay stable for Paige, but my own volatile emotions were roiling right beneath the surface.

Murderous.

Fucking.

Wrath.

All I really wanted was to see Justin Talmage suffer. But his rich daddy had fucking protected him. The spineless puke had preyed on someone without his family's power, a woman who had still dreamed of meeting a man she loved.

Not only had that bastard raped her body, but he'd stripped her of her innocence in more ways than one.

Christ! Had I once been a spoiled, rich bastard like he was? I immediately discounted that errant, angry thought. I might have been a guy who was drifting, but I sure as hell had never drugged and fucked an unwilling female. I'd gotten laid plenty, but it was completely consensual.

I looked down at Paige, a woman who'd been completely destroyed by what Talmage had done to her, but who had also gotten back up to keep fighting for her life. And dammit...she *was* successful, despite her internal torment. One look at her grades at Harvard and the fact that she'd also had to support herself while making those perfect grades made me feel like a damn slacker.

Finally, I swallowed my intense reaction and asked, "Did you need medical treatment?"

Oh, Jesus. Please say no!

"It hurt so badly that I was thankful for the times when the drugs he gave me made the pain go away. But I didn't go to the hospital afterward. I could barely walk, and I woke up back at my place covered in so much blood it scared me. All I could think of was that I had to shower away the ugliness and dirtiness, then get out of my apartment. When I said he raped me, I meant in every possible way," she shared quietly.

I fucking knew what she meant. He'd shoved his dick up her ass, too, and she'd bled from everywhere. "What did you do?"

"Luckily, I healed. The pain went away. I went to the only people I trusted...my parents."

And her folks hadn't given her the reassurance she'd needed back then. Jesus, that made my chest ache like hell. "So you've never actually had a boyfriend?"

She cocked an eyebrow at me for beating around the bush. "What you want to ask is if I ever had sex again."

Paige was correct. I did want to know. "Yes."

"I tried. I didn't want to be emotionally involved, but I searched for a man who could make me feel something good once I was in law school and had gone through some counseling."

"And?"

She lowered her head. "I didn't feel anything. If your next question is if I've ever had an orgasm, I haven't. I think I'm sexually dysfunctional. I just don't bother to try anymore."

So, she'd had a few fumbling college dudes try to make her feel pleasure instead of pain, and she hadn't. "I can make you come, Paige," I said, my voice hoarse with the need to touch her, see her body's response as she screamed out my name when she found release. This woman deserved to see that sex wasn't always bad. And I sure as hell needed to be the one to show her that.

For some reason, I'd always had the desperate urge to see her while she was in the throes of a massive orgasm.

Paige shook her head. "I've given up trying. And even though I have to admit I'm attracted to you, I can't have sex with you. That would make things complicated."

"They don't have to be."

She slipped out of my arms, and I felt the loss immediately.

"Sebastian, you're the owner of Walker. I'm a junior attorney. I want this job."

"Do you? You said business law wasn't your first choice."

"It's all I have," she mumbled, still not looking up.

Her melancholy response hit me square in the gut and left me wanting to tell her she fucking had *me*.

I knew damn well getting intimate would complicate our lives, but I didn't care. I fucking *wanted* things to get complicated as hell. For the first time in my life, all I wanted was one woman… her. No female had ever made me react this way, and I wasn't sure I liked it. But I was *damn* sure that I couldn't ignore it.

"Sex only," I suggested, lying my ass off. "No strings for one month. If I can't make you come, you can dump me. I won't mix business with pleasure. No bad feelings on either side. We could call it an experiment."

She was silenced by my offer, and I could practically see what she was thinking by the changing expressions on her face. She was thinking about it, but I wasn't at all sure she was going to take me up on my offer.

Honestly, it was purely selfish. I wanted to get my hands on Paige Rutledge, but I knew once I did, it *was* going to get complicated. Once she was mine, I'd be as fucking possessive of her as my brother was with Eva. Hell, I was already well on my way.

Problem was, I didn't want to scare her off. My gut ached from wanting to make her feel important, desirable, and to be the guy she'd run to when she needed anything.

"I can't," she whispered, barely loud enough to hear.

I moved forward and pinned her against the vanity, resting one hand on each side of the counter so she couldn't scurry away. My grip was so hard on the granite that my knuckles were white.

Her running and hiding days were fucking over. That behavior *wasn't* Paige; it was her history.

"You can. Say yes," I cajoled. "Let me show you how it can be."

I wasn't shy about my skills at making women orgasm. I'd certainly done enough perfecting of those talents over the years. And the chemistry between me and Paige was combustible.

Not able to stop myself, I leaned down to kiss her so thoroughly that her brain would stop thinking and her body would respond to me. At least I hoped it would.

It was a kiss made to tease, tempt, and get the answer from her that I wanted. My heart hammered as she opened herself to me, wrapping her arms around my neck and started giving as good as she got.

Relief flooded through my tense muscles. There was no way I was going to push her any harder. She had to make this *her* choice. But I was sure as hell willing to persuade her without crossing the line.

My cock was hard enough to cut diamonds as she moaned against my lips, her body trembling as I nibbled on her lower lip, then her neck, pushing my groin into her body to let her know exactly how I was reacting. "I want you, Paige," I confessed. "I always have."

"Sebastian," she said on a sigh, leaning her head back to give more access to the sensitive skin I needed to claim. "Yes."

It was the one word I really wanted to hear. I doubted that she was agreeing to our arrangement, but I'd pretend she did for now.

At that moment, I was desperate enough to do anything. "I can make it good for you." It would either be explosive for her, or I'd die trying.

"Sex only," she moaned.

"Yeah," I agreed readily. Sex for now. Everything else could be figured out later.

"Yes." She moaned again as I grabbed her ass and pulled her against me. "But just for tonight."

"Not tonight." It was painful to say those words as I breathed in her fresh, clean fragrance. Even though I knew I probably didn't have her shampoo, damned if she didn't still have the same seductive scent.

She rubbed her soft cheek against my stubble, just like a cat that brushed their coat along people or convenient surfaces. "Tonight," she demanded. "*Just* tonight. Then we get this out of our systems and move on."

I kissed her again, needing to somehow make this woman belong to me. I needed her in ways that were unexplainable. Yeah, I had to possess her body. But there was so much more... "No, baby. Not after what you've been through tonight."

"I need you, Sebastian."

Jesus! She could never need me as much as I needed her. "I'm not agreeing to one night. There's no way I won't want to fuck you tomorrow, and the next day, then the day after that." It was all I thought about lately. This was more than getting laid to me.

"It's all I can agree to," she answered in a voice full of regret.

Maybe it was all she could promise, but I'd get more. I had to. "Tonight," I half-ass agreed, not bothering to mention that I didn't plan on making this a one-night stand.

"I feel a little nervous," she admitted boldly. "It's been a long time."

"If you didn't get off, it's been forever," I told her gruffly, then I scooped her up and carried her out the doorway of the room I'd given her to use and headed down the hallway. If this surreal wet dream was going to become reality, it was happening in my bed. "Don't be afraid of me, sweetheart. Please don't be scared. I'd never hurt you."

One of the reasons I hadn't wanted to claim her tonight was because I knew she was still recovering from reliving what happened with Justin.

"I'm not afraid of you," she replied.

Okay, that was *something*. "Don't be nervous, either. I just want to make you feel good."

She sighed and laid her head on my shoulder, an action of trust that nearly made my damn chest explode as she replied, "I'm not your usual glamorous female with tons of experience. I'm more afraid of disappointing you."

Okay. *That* comment was like a knife to my gut. Paige had me twisted inside out, and she was afraid she wouldn't make me happy? "Just being with you makes me happy, sweetheart," I answered huskily as I walked into my own bedroom.

"Why?"

I couldn't tell her how I really felt, how connected I'd been to her almost from the moment we met. I lusted after her, I respected her, I admired her courage, and I damn well adored her spirit.

I shrugged off her question. "We understand each other," I answered simply.

She frowned as I set her on her feet. "Do we? I'm not sure I always get what you want from me."

Everything!

Yeah, I couldn't admit that to her or she'd go running for the door. But I wanted it all. The complications, the laughter that she so seldom let leave her beautiful lips, her genuine smile, her inquisitive questions, her body, her heart, and her goddamn soul.

I knew I was becoming just like the green monster that Trace was with his wife, but I'd eat every word I'd ever said to him if I could just have Paige.

"Right now, I just want you naked," I told her bluntly.

I had to swallow a lump in my throat as she began to comply.

CHAPTER 13

Paige

*A*ll I had to do was lift the nightgown over my head and I'd be as naked as the day I was born.

I started the action, then hesitated.

What in the hell am I doing? There's no way I can just screw him tonight and forget about it tomorrow.

But I was so tired of running away from everything that scared me, or just avoiding it altogether. The emptiness inside me ran deep, and all I wanted was one night for myself, one night to replace the memories that kept flashing through my mind.

Sebastian wanted my body.

I wanted to feel pleasure.

It should be the perfect situation.

But I knew it was not.

I was starting to care about him, and I didn't screw men who were an emotional danger to me. Not that I'd ever met one before. Sebastian was a new kind of temptation, and I was rapidly losing all rational thought.

Right now, I just wanted to lose myself in *him*, and forget that I was vulnerable.

For once, I was ready to be selfish and spontaneous.

I yanked the garment over my head and tossed it on the floor. I was going to do this, and I was going to relish every moment of it.

He quickly jerked his T-shirt over his head, a gesture that he was as willing to bare himself to me, just like I was doing for him.

My mouth watered as I blatantly stared at the abundance of smooth skin that covered the hard muscles of his chest, biceps, and abdomen.

Sweet Jesus! Sebastian took my breath away and I hadn't even touched him yet.

Generally, I'd want to cover my body, but if Sebastian was going to show me pleasure, he'd get to know every generous curve intimately before this night was over. He might as well look and see what he was getting into.

The heat in his eyes reassured and surprised me, so I moved forward and boldly yanked on the tie on his gray sweatpants. "Lose them," I demanded, eager to get my first glance at what I already knew was going to be a stunningly gorgeous sight. His chest was broad and smooth, muscular and strong. Obviously, he was very active in sports, or he worked out. Considering how much he worked, and how large his house was, I assumed he had a home gym.

I stepped back and watched as he lowered the pants, revealing what was beneath that tantalizing trail of sandy brown hair that went from below his belly button and mysteriously disappeared inside the waistband of his sweatpants. His eyes never left me as he kicked off the last garment that was preventing me from gawking at him in all his glory.

And I did stare at him shamelessly for a period of time I couldn't even identify. All I knew was that he was so incredibly masculine and perfect that I could hardly draw a breath.

The hard lines on his face and clenched fists made me realize he was waiting. He was going to let me make the first move.

Maybe he was afraid of scaring me, but fear was the last thing on my mind right now.

My body reacted, my core flooding with heat as I stepped forward and finally laid my palms on his chest, reveling in the feel of his heated skin. My hands traced the muscles on his chest before I moved them down to follow that tantalizing trail of hair that led down to one enormous cock.

I was drowning in sensation just from the feel of his body, and I couldn't wait to feel our connection skin-to-skin. Tentatively, I wrapped my fingers around his shaft, stroking the silky skin over his hardness. I'd never really had the chance to fondle a man, and the freedom to touch him was exhilarating.

I traced over the head, swiping up the drop of moisture that was beaded there, then lifted my finger to my mouth, dying to taste him.

I closed my eyes as I sucked his essence from my finger, savoring a taste that was so much like his scent: masculine, seductive, and absolutely delicious.

"Fuck!" Sebastian shouted. "If you do that one more time, I don't think I can resist touching you. I want to give you time. Let you get used to my body. But I don't think I can handle this much longer."

I looked up at him, and the tumultuous look on his face spurred me on. I wanted him to touch me. While I appreciated his restraint for my sake, it was completely unnecessary. I wasn't afraid of Sebastian; I wanted to immerse myself in him, let myself be swept away.

I put my finger to his steely cock, stroked it, then put my finger to his slit to grab a bead of moisture before putting my finger to my lips. Before I licked my finger, I locked eyes with him and said in a teasing voice, "Then I guess you're going to have to touch me." I flicked out my tongue and savored his taste again.

"Goddamn it, Paige. I want to be patient—"

"Don't," I pleaded. "Don't treat me like a fragile flower. I'm not. Fuck me like you would any other woman offering herself up to you."

"You aren't any other woman," he answered in a graveled voice. "You're different. You've always been different. I'm not taking you down and dirty like you're just another fuck."

I could tell he was thoroughly aroused, but holding back because he wanted me to feel comfortable. *Screw comfortable!* I was on fire, my body starting to tremble with an unsatisfied need that I'd never experienced before.

I wrapped my arms around his neck and threaded my fingers through his thick locks of hair. "I might like down and dirty," I argued. "All I know is if you don't start touching me, I'm going to burn alive."

Finally, I pressed my body into his and yanked his head down to kiss him, moaning against his lips as our fiery skin fused together in the most exquisite pleasure I'd ever experienced.

"Fuck it!" Sebastian said, right before his steely arms wrapped around my waist and he took total control of the embrace, his tongue piercing into my mouth with a surge of dominance that made me even hotter.

Suddenly, his hands were everywhere. He stroked them over my ass and up my back, then back down again, changing positions over and over, like he didn't want to leave one inch of my skin untouched.

My body melted in pleasure as his kiss grew insistent and demanding, his hands urgent and needy. I moved my fingers from his hair to his shoulders, stroking and exploring, just like he was doing to me. My nipples were hard and sensitive, and every movement of his body just increased the sensual abrasion of the tips against his hard body.

We kissed and touched like we were desperate, like connecting with each other was integral to our survival. He finally pulled his mouth from mine and nipped at my bottom lip, then soothed it with his tongue before he began to nuzzle the sensitive skin of my neck.

"Jesus, Paige. You feel even better than my fantasies," he rasped against my neck.

I shivered as he ran his tongue over my sensitive earlobe, and I could feel his hot breath against my ear.

"I didn't know you had fantasies about me," I gasped.

"Tons of them," he answered as he moved forward, pushing me toward his massive bed. "I've fucked you at least a hundred times in my mind since we met."

My thighs hit the edge of the bed, and Sebastian lifted me into his arms and tossed me gently into the middle of the soft comforter. He was on me, planting soft kisses on my mouth, before I could miss the heat of his body.

"Was it good for you?" I teased as he pinned my hands over my head gently.

"This is a hell of a lot better," he said in a throaty, low drawl right beside my ear, the heated declaration making a trail of heat slither down my spine.

His mouth moved lower, finally brushing against a sensitive nipple as he demanded, "Don't touch me. Not now. Just relax."

He released my wrists and slid lower, his hands cupping my breasts. His hands moved over the outer edges, his fingers moving closer and closer in a lazy circular motion toward the almost painfully hard peaks.

When his mouth finally descended to cover one of my nipples, I cried out in relief as pleasure flooded my body. "Yes," I moaned. "Please."

He teased and alternated from breast to breast, slowly making me so crazy that I closed my eyes and arched my back.

"Patience, baby," he drawled right before his tongue slid lower and he teased his way down my body.

"I've waited almost twenty-seven years," I reminded him loudly, spearing my hands into his hair to make him move faster.

I heard his amused chuckle as he moved between my thighs and eased them apart to accommodate his large body.

"Relax," he crooned again. "You don't need to do a damn thing except come."

I suddenly realized that he was lowering his head between my thighs.

My body writhed, demanding satisfaction. "No. I don't do that. Just fuck me," I begged.

He ignored me and positioned himself so he was exactly where he wanted to be. "Never? Well, damn, sweetheart. You've definitely missed something that feels good."

I sighed. I wouldn't know what it felt like to have a guy go down on me. I'd never had it, and I wasn't sure I wanted to start now. My body was aching, begging for…something. I was pretty sure it was for Sebastian to come back to me and give me what I needed.

My entire body jerked as I felt his slick tongue spear through my quivering flesh, connecting briefly with my clit. "Oh, God."

He didn't go slow. He boldly devoured my pussy like a man who needed it to keep breathing. His tongue lapped eagerly at my juices, and I jolted every time he connected with the sensitive bundle of nerves begging for attention.

"That feels so good," I cried out, my hands twisting in the silky cover on the bed.

I closed my eyes as he gave my clit the pressure I didn't know it needed, and then slipped a finger into my slick channel.

He finger-fucked me gently at first, but as I became hotter and wetter, he added a second finger into my tight channel, and his tongue started a mind-blowing rhythm centered on my clit.

A knot of warmth started to unfurl in my belly, and it radiated down to where Sebastian was playing my body like it was an instrument that he mastered.

"Sebastian," I moaned. "Yes. Harder."

He accommodated me, and I speared my fingers into his hair and held his head against my pussy as my entire body started to go up in flames.

My first orgasm didn't come softly. The damn thing plowed through my body like a steamroller as wave after wave of sensation and heat pummeled me. I screamed out as I arched my back in the pleasure/pain of my explosive release. "Sebastian! Yes. Yes."

I was yanking on his hair as the painful part ended and the pleasure lingered in ripples that overwhelmed my senses.

My legs were quivering, and my satiated body was covered in a mist of sweat as Sebastian continued to lick my pussy until he'd greedily lapped up every drop of fluid that had flooded my core as I'd climaxed.

I couldn't think.

I couldn't move.

I couldn't quite process what had just happened, so I just let the post-climatic pleasure stay with me as I gasped for breath.

I clung to Sebastian as he crawled up my body, wrapping my arms so tightly around his neck that I couldn't be sure I wasn't cutting off his air.

"Thank you," I gasped, still short of breath. "Oh, God, that was amazing."

He kissed me tenderly, and I tasted myself on his lips.

When he lifted his head, I saw the turbulent fire in his eyes and our gazes connected. "It wasn't exactly a sacrifice, Paige. I've imagined you like this since the moment I saw you," he answered huskily.

It was hard to imagine that Sebastian had experienced insta-lust for me the first time we'd met on the elevator. "I was a bitch the first time we met."

"Didn't matter. I recognized you anyway," he answered hoarsely, his eyes filled with an incendiary heat that made me instinctively lift my body to rub up against him.

I wasn't certain exactly what he meant, but my mind wasn't processing much at the moment. Unable to resist being skin-to-skin with him again, I wrapped my arms around his big body and tried to pull him down to rest on top of me.

"I don't want to fuck you, Paige. Not tonight," he rasped, his body tense again from holding back.

"You will fuck me, Mr. Walker, or I'll never forgive you. I've waited forever for this." Yes, I was still in post-orgasmic bliss. But the empty places inside me still existed, and I knew I wouldn't be completely sated until Sebastian had been elementally joined to me. I needed to feel him be a part of me, if only for a brief amount of time.

The corners of his mouth started to turn up like he was fighting a smile as he answered, "Jesus! I love that dirty professional voice."

His mouth came down on mine with a breathtaking passion that I could only assume he'd just let loose.

My spirit soared, and I wrapped my legs around his legs instinctively, practically climbing up on his body and begging him to fuck me without saying a word.

He threaded a hand between us, and said in a torture voice, "I shouldn't do this tonight."

"Fuck me, Sebastian," I murmured into his ear, urging him on, my body so damn primed for him that I held my breath, silently begging him to enter me.

Tonight was all we had, and I wanted it all, everything he had to give.

I gasped as he invaded my tight sheath with one forceful thrust. I knew he was big, and I'd been prepared for that. What I hadn't foreseen was just how amazing it would feel to have him buried to his balls inside my body, my muscles stretching to accommodate his size, my heart racing because I finally felt...free.

"Sebastian," I muttered, nearly incoherent as he gripped my ass tightly and pulled back only to return with another powerful surge. "Yes. Please. Fuck me."

"I can't hold back, Paige," he said in a tormented tone.

"Don't. Please don't. I want everything."

I wanted to experience the wonder of actually enjoying sex, and I knew Sebastian was the only man who could give me that, give me all that I'd missed.

"Fuck. Paige," he groaned as he slammed into me again and again, like he needed my body like a dehydrated mammal needed water.

He was just that passionate, that greedy and desperate.

And he caught me up in his fire, my body like tinder to his flame. Once ignited, I couldn't stop.

I caught his punishing rhythm and rose to meet every thrust, my heart racing, my breath short and shallow as our perspiring bodies reached for the same goal together.

"I need you, Sebastian. I need you so much. Don't stop," I cried out as I tightened my legs around him, wishing the ecstasy of being with him could go on and on.

He gripped my ass tighter as he growled, "I want to get so deep inside you that you never forget how it feels when I'm fucking you."

He pulled my body up tightly against him with his grip on my rear, and I strained to accept everything he had.

"I could never forget," I whimpered.

"Come for me, baby," he demanded coarsely.

I could feel the same coil of blistering heat flooding my body, but I didn't fly over the top until Sebastian grasped my hair and positioned my head so he could kiss me. His other hand slid between our tight bodies and he thumbed my clit, setting off my body like a firecracker on the Fourth of July.

My climax sizzled through my being, my core clamping down on his cock as waves of pleasure cascaded through me.

I screamed the moment Sebastian lifted his head after his impassioned kiss. "Yesssss!" I hissed at the end of my howl of ecstasy.

"Paige!" Sebastian groaned as he reared up and buried himself inside my tight, spasming sheath over and over again.

His face was fierce, his expression tortured when he finally found his release, his prolonged groan of pleasure as he threw his head back was one of the rawest things I'd ever witnessed. The corded muscles in his neck were flexing, and his chest was slick and covered with sweat. But to see him at an intimate moment like we were experiencing was breathtakingly beautiful. There was no other way to describe him.

I wallowed in his pleasure as it mingled with mine, our bodies both shuddering with relief.

Untangling our limbs, Sebastian rolled off me and gathered me into his arms as we caught our breath.

He didn't say anything as we struggled to recover, but the silence was broken by our ragged breaths, and I could feel my heart pumping as it eventually started to slow down.

One of his hands was stroking over my back, and in that moment, I found a peace like I hadn't known since...well... maybe never.

Eventually, we stirred, and Sebastian laid a gentle kiss on my lips and started caressing my hair so naturally that I wasn't even sure he knew he was doing it.

I buried my face in his warm chest, then laid my head on it. "Thank you," I said again, at a loss for words at the moment. What else could I say to the man who had just rocked my whole world?

"Still think you're sexually dysfunctional?" he said in a teasing tone.

"Probably not," I agreed with a smile.

"We might have a small problem, though," he mused.

"What?" I couldn't think of one thing that hadn't been perfect.

"I didn't use a condom, Paige," he muttered remorsefully. "I don't want you to hate me if you end up pregnant."

CHAPTER 14

Paige

I hadn't even thought about protection. There were other reasons why we should have used a condom other than the possibility of me getting knocked up. "I'm on the pill. I have been since Justin raped me."

I shuddered. After that experience, and the anxiety of waiting to see if I was pregnant, I knew I never wanted to go through that again.

His body had tensed, and I felt him physically relax. "I should have stopped."

"I wasn't going to let you," I answered, perfectly willing to take the blame. "I was checked for any diseases after the attack. Then again after my last sexual encounter during my routine checkup, even though he wore a condom. I'm clean of any STDs. I haven't been with anyone since then."

"I was a man-whore up until I came to Denver. But I was checked, too. I've never not used a condom. I don't even keep them around anymore since they just collect dust. I know I can't expect you to believe me, but I can get the medical records."

I leaned back so I could see his face. "I believe you."

He gave me a puzzled look. "Why?"

I laughed as I gazed at his confused expression. "Why wouldn't I? You've been honest with me so far."

"Because I lived a high-risk lifestyle."

"And you always wore a condom. You got checked." I stroked his whiskered jaw. "Sebastian, I encouraged you. I didn't stop to think about diseases, and I should have. I think you would have stopped if you thought you were risking my health. I know I would have told you before things had gone that far."

"I lost count of how many women I've had. Honestly, I was usually so far under the influence that I can barely remember most of my sexual encounters during those years," he admitted, sounding regretful.

"I. Don't. Care." I said each word distinctly. Yeah, maybe I should have mentioned a condom. But I knew I wasn't going to get pregnant, and I was getting to know Sebastian well enough to know he wouldn't knowingly hurt me in *any* way. "If anyone should be scared, it's you. You had no idea that I was on birth control."

He was silent for a moment before he answered, "Well, I guess we're safe."

Sebastian didn't address why he hadn't been worried if I got pregnant, but I didn't ask. We'd both gotten caught up in the moment, and that was all there was to our mistake.

Honestly, I'd been so zoned out to everything except Sebastian that it was almost frightening.

I sighed and cuddled against him again. "I really didn't know it could be like that."

"Me either," he answered in a husky voice.

"You've been with plenty of other women," I reminded him.

"Not like that." I felt his chin brush against my hair as he shook his head.

He tightened his arms around me possessively as I answered, "I might get better with more practice."

"Round two?" he asked, his voice amused. "Not happening tonight, sweetheart. You're going to be hurting in muscles you forgot you had in the morning. I feel like shit that I got so rough, but I plead insanity, counselor."

"Tonight is all we have," I said, hating the plea in my voice. I sounded pathetic, but if I was never going to be with Sebastian again, I wanted…more.

"No, it's not. Sleep," he suggested as he buried his face in my hair. "You have to be exhausted."

I was tired, but my body was still zinging with leftover adrenaline.

He bodily lifted me and turned me around so he was spooning me, one strong, possessive arm around my waist. It was an intimate position, but it felt good to have our bodies plastered together again.

I let out a long sigh of contentment. "I noticed that almost all of the women's clothing in the closet still has tags on them." I was curious, but I didn't want to outright ask him why they were there.

"My aunt Aileen stays with me now when she comes to Denver on business. She doesn't get here often, but since Trace is married, she says she's more comfortable staying here with me. That's her favorite room, and she ordered the clothes so she'd never have to pack if she came here. She hasn't needed to stay here since she stocked the closet."

"She's Blake Colter's mother," I murmured, remembering her name from my research.

"Not just Blake's. She has other kids."

"I know. One daughter and four boys. Tate, Chloe, Zane, Blake, and Marcus."

"Jesus! Do you have a photographic memory or what?"

I smiled. "Not that I know of, but I do remember most of what I read."

"Hell, sometimes I can't remember the names of people I've met before, much less people who mean nothing to me," he grumbled.

"It's a skill I picked up from working and going to school. My study time was a little hampered by my jobs. I had to retain everything I read." I paused before asking, "So did I remember right?"

"Yeah. That's all of them. My aunt Aileen is the woman who keeps them all in line. She runs the resort I mentioned in Rocky Springs."

"Do you mind when she stays with you?"

"Not at all. I'm hardly ever here, and if she stays with me, she cooks."

I laughed softly. "So you actually eat."

"She's one hell of a cook. Yeah, I definitely eat."

"I hope she doesn't get mad that I borrowed her nightgown."

"She won't. She'd offer you the shirt off her back if you needed it. She's a good, kind woman," Sebastian assured me.

I was silent as I processed my disappointment that my body wasn't going to come apart again tonight, but then I savored the sensation of having Sebastian's powerful body against my back. He threw off heat, and kept me warm and secure as I contemplated the repercussions of what had happened this evening.

No doubt, meeting up with him at work would be awkward, but if we were both professional, we'd manage.

The steady breath hitting the back of my neck told me Sebastian had fallen asleep, his arm still wrapped as tightly around me in sleep as it had been when he was awake.

One glance at the large windows told me the sun was rising. No wonder Sebastian had fallen asleep. I was exhausted, too, but my mind kept playing different scenarios over and over again.

My heart squeezed like a tight fist was wrapped around the organ, a crushing pain heavy on my chest.

Morning had come, and my fantasy night was over.

Problem was, Sebastian Walker had made me feel all of the things my mom always said I would, but he was unattainable.

Not only was he the owner of Walker Enterprises, but he was obviously obsessed with work.

He wasn't relationship material, and neither was I.

A lone tear trickled down my cheek as I kept on savoring how good he felt, how right it was that he'd been the man to finally show me how pleasurable intimacy could be.

I can't have more!

This night had been my fling, my one-night stand to chase away some of the ghosts that haunted me. Strangely enough, it had worked. Knowing I wasn't incapable of having a climax opened up an entirely different door for me. It wasn't that I hadn't tried to achieve an orgasm myself, but I'd never quite gotten there. Now, I surmised that I'd just been trying too hard. I'd been trying to prove that it was possible instead of just relaxing and letting it happen. Eventually, I'd gotten frustrated and given up.

Now that I know it's possible, I think I can get myself off.

The ache in my chest was still there, even though I'd opened a part of myself tonight that I'd never looked at, much less shared before. Sebastian had said this night wasn't the last time, but he hadn't been thinking straight.

It *had* to be the only time.

I wasn't about to become a fuck buddy to him, and he meant more than that to me.

I'm falling for him.

I sighed as I finally admitted the truth. Sebastian Walker moved me in ways I never thought possible. We fit. We connected. In superficial ways, we couldn't be more different. But we'd shared a lot of the same issues in different ways, and I'd never forget his kindness to me when I needed it the most.

But the naked truth was…Sebastian didn't do relationships, and neither did I. Hell, I wasn't even sure I knew how. I'd been alone for so long that I didn't understand how to be with anybody.

Maybe if I cared a little less, we could use each other to scratch an itch occasionally. But I'd be lying if I convinced myself that being with him casually wouldn't hurt me. In time, it very well might destroy me.

Somehow, I needed to consider this night a learning experience and try to forget that Sebastian Walker had rocked my world so profoundly that I'd never be the same again.

Not that I regretted what happened. I didn't. I knew exactly what I was doing. But to expect anything more was pointless.

Take what you learned and grow from it.

Slowly, as the light of day started filtering in from the cracks in the blinds, I began to rebuild my strength.

I eased out of Sebastian's tight hold without waking him, knowing my first line of protection was distance.

I don't want to wake up and have everything feel awkward between us.

I needed time to think.

I walked naked into the bedroom that Sebastian had originally showed me to and picked up my dress and my clutch bag. The gown was ruined. The moisture stains causing portions of the garment to fade. I fumbled with my bag and pulled out my cell phone to call a taxi before I purloined a pair of jeans and a sweater from the collection of clothes in the closet.

I'll replace them.

I planned on going to the store and replacing what I'd used.

Using the stairs instead of the elevator, I briefly looked around his place as I made my way back to the kitchen, stunned as I discovered each new room. Not only did he have a complete gym, but he also possessed an indoor pool, and more bedroom suites than I could count. I wasn't surprised when I found a theater room for movies, and a game room that had a pool table that looked like it was rarely used.

The whole house was breathtaking without being ostentatious. Obviously, it was a home meant to be used and loved.

I found my heels near the kitchen, exactly where I'd kicked them off, and I forced my bare feet into the high stilettos before I glanced longingly up toward the place where Sebastian still slept.

I didn't want to leave him. I didn't want to go. But my safety mechanisms were firmly in place, and I knew that I had to fondly remember this night without letting my feelings for Sebastian take me over. If I did, I knew I'd never survive.

I wrote a quick, terse note to him, thanking him for helping me, and letting him know that I couldn't stay because I had other obligations this morning. It was a blatant lie, but my blasé communication sounded just how I meant him to interpret it: a brush off and a reminder that this was a one-night-only thing.

I let myself out from the garage, pushing the button again and racing to get clear before the solid metal door clanged shut with a finality that wrenched at my soul.

Done.

Finished.

My interlude with Sebastian could never be more than just a fond memory.

I swept one last tear from my face as the taxi pulled up to Sebastian's house, and I hopped in, resisting the urge to look back as the car pulled away to take me home.

I was back at my place when I realized that I only had one of my earrings still affixed to my left ear. The other one was gone. Maybe it was just a fairly inexpensive piece of jewelry, but it was my most sentimental connection to my mom. Really, one of the only things I still had left from her.

Leaving Sebastian had been one of the hardest things I'd ever done, but staying and facing him in the morning would have made leaving even harder. But I was feeling the same emptiness creep up inside me again, and losing that fragile connection with my mother was the last straw.

Alone in my apartment, I carefully removed the other earring, sat on my sofa, and wept.

CHAPTER 15

Sebastian

"*I* got what was coming to me, I guess," I told Trace on Monday morning as I slumped in the chair in front of his desk on the top floor. "The player finally got played."

I'll never forget how I felt waking up alone two mornings ago. First, I panicked because she was gone. Then, I worried about her being safe. Finally, I found the note Paige had left on the kitchen counter while I ran through the house like a lunatic screaming her name over and over again. After that, I went into a state somewhere between anger and despair. I'm thinking at one point I slipped over a line closer to anger, because I wanted to smash every single thing that I could get into my hand to release my furious disappointment.

I hadn't held back with Trace this morning. I'd told him everything. I was fucking sick of pretending that I wasn't obsessed with Paige Rutledge. I'd glossed over some of the more intimate details, but he knew all the basics.

Trace leaned back in his chair as he donned a thoughtful expression. "I can't believe that son of a bitch, Talmage, got away with raping a woman."

"I can," I said irritably. "How often have we seen money buy somebody out of trouble? How often has the power of being rich made a man think he's above everyone else?"

"I have to admit, I pulled a few strings for Eva, but nothing like this, and she was innocent."

I could never compare my oldest brother to Talmage in any way. "Everybody knows somebody. This was flat-out arrogance and Talmage thinking he'd never pay for what he did because his daddy has money."

Trace nodded. "We might be rich, but we can thank Dad for teaching us that we're no better than anyone else, and being wealthy comes with the responsibility of helping others as much as we possibly can."

"He taught us by example," I agreed. My father had been one of the most generous, kindest men I'd ever known. He'd never used his power to intimidate other people. He was a businessman, but he was also very human.

One of the reasons I'd straightened my ass out was because I knew my father would be disappointed in the way I'd acted. I'd been the spoiled, obnoxious asshole that my dad had abhorred.

"We need to take the bastard down," Trace said angrily. "It needs to be done for every woman who has ever been hurt by Talmage. And we need to do it for Paige."

I looked at the furious expression on my brother's face, knowing damn well he was thinking about Eva, and how helpless his wife had once been. "I'd rather just kill the bastard, but I'd have to find him first. It seems he's left Colorado."

Trace raised a questioning brow. "You looked for him?"

I nodded. "Yesterday. I drove back to see his father. All he'd tell me was that his son had gone out of state."

"What did you do about the property?"

"I told him to shove it up his ass. I'm not doing business with some prick who probably knows his son is a loser, but defends him anyway." I inhaled a sharp breath as my anger started to rise to danger level. "I'll find another location."

Trace leaned forward and braced his forearms on his desk. "I don't care about the property, Sebastian. There are other parcels of land. I'm worried about you. I know what it's like to deal with a woman who was treated like shit and didn't deserve it. It almost ate me alive."

"What in the hell did you do? How do you handle something like that?"

Trace grimaced. "I had to think about Eva and all that she'd been through. My goal was, and still is, to make her happy. Her self-esteem was understandably low, and not a goddamn soul had given a shit that she was paying for something she didn't do."

I could hear the indignation vibrating through Trace's tone, and I knew he was still majorly pissed that a wonderful woman like Eva had been through so much alone.

Sadly, I could completely relate. "I feel the same way about Paige. She had nobody after she disagreed with her parents. Dammit! She had the right to prosecute the bastard."

"She did," Trace agreed readily. "But I think she probably realizes now that she never would have won. It's not fair, but it would basically be her word against a rich man's son. There was no proof."

Logically, I knew that. Hell, I wasn't sure if her parents even believed her. But it still made me crazy. "I think she realizes that now that she's an attorney. She basically said she'd never have won the case."

"But you're still angry," Trace said, giving his brother a knowing look.

"Hell, yeah. I hate the idea of anyone even touching Paige, much less violating her," I growled, trying not to think about any man putting a hand on Paige.

"You're toast," Trace said flatly. "You're gone. Once you start feeling like that, it's over, Sebastian."

I glared at him. "What's over?"

Trace grinned. "Your days as a player. Eventually, she'll haunt you until you can't stay away."

"Already there," I admitted through a jaw clenched with irritation. "But she left that damn note, and I'm not going to keep chasing her like a crazy-ass stalker. It's pretty obvious that she doesn't want anything more to do with me."

"Bullshit," Trace shot back. "She didn't give you her trust easily. No woman in her position would. She's either scared, or she thinks she's not good enough for you. In your case, I'd say it's a little of both."

I tried to think rationally, wondering if there wasn't some truth in what my brother was saying. "You think she's afraid I'll hurt her, or I was just using her?"

Trace shrugged. "Defense mechanisms in women who have had it rough are pretty damn strong. Think about it. She's had to struggle for every damn thing in her life. She felt betrayed by her own parents, and she's entirely focused on her career because she wants to feel safe."

"She's hiding," I answered, once again getting the feeling that Paige had conditioned herself to be so damn anally disciplined. "She's always been hiding. I could sense it, even the first time we met."

"So find *her*," Trace suggested firmly. "Don't let her hide."

"I did find her," I admitted. "But then I lost her again."

"She's still there. She's just afraid," Trace said slowly. "You know damn well you want to hunt her down and make her realize that you aren't just playing with her."

"My playing days are over," I said gruffly. "They have been since the day I met her. Even before that, actually, but Paige made me realize it."

"Then help her heal. Get in her face. If you think she feels the same way you do, don't just give up."

I straightened up in my chair. "How the hell do I know how she feels? She's grateful. She thanked me. But I feel like she just blew me off. I actually got drunk yesterday for the first in over a year."

Trace frowned. "Are you okay?"

"I'm fine. I took one day to escape. I'm not going to go back to my old habits."

"Don't let this eat you up, man. Wouldn't it be better to know you tried than to just let her go?" Trace ask solemnly. "I still say no woman trusts a guy with everything if they don't care about him."

My anger started to dissolve as I remembered the way Paige had trusted me with her body, even after she had every reason to never have faith in a guy again. She'd accepted the drink I'd poured without question, even after her painful flashback. "Yeah, she has to feel something," I acknowledged.

"You can be a major pain in the ass when you want to be," Trace drawled, his comment sounding like a hint.

I looked at him as he leaned back in his chair with a quizzical expression.

I nodded. "I can."

"Persistence pays off. But you already know that. It just has to be something or somebody worth fighting for."

"She's worth whatever battle I have to fight," I answered, my voice raw with emotion. Maybe I'd never quite admitted how I felt to myself, but Trace knew. If I thought she'd be happy if I just backed off, I'd do it. But I knew my brother was right. I'd have to get in her face to help her really heal. It was so much easier to just run away to a safe, familiar place than to face demons that you didn't want to fight.

"I'm here if you need help," Trace replied supportively.

"She's stubborn and scared," I said, thinking out loud.

"You're one of the most pigheaded men I know," Trace said jokingly.

I smirked back at him. "That trait might come in handy right now."

"Just try to win her over before Thanksgiving. Eva wants to meet the woman who finally grabbed you by the balls. She worries about you and Dane."

I started thinking about my plan of attack, knowing there was no way Paige was going to keep pushing me away unless she really *didn't* want me. "Maybe Eva should give Paige a call. Invite her to Thanksgiving dinner? Seeing as Paige is here with no family or friends."

Trace grinned. "She'd be up for that. Besides the fact that she wants to meet the woman who got your attention, she's so damn softhearted that if she knew Paige was alone here in Denver without family or friends, she'd be on the phone in a heartbeat."

Eva had once been just as alone as Paige. I knew I could count on my sister-in-law to call Paige and invite her to dinner. "Thanks," I muttered to my brother. "I'll handle the rest."

"I'm sure you will," Trace responded.

I was quiet as I thought about the work I had ahead of me today. "I'm sorry about the setback on the solar build."

"It's not your fault," Trace answered, sounding confused. "I wouldn't do business with the bastard, either."

"I think I have another possibility. I'll get on it." I rose out of my chair to get my ass into my own office.

"Sebastian?"

I turned when Trace said my name. "Yeah?"

"Some things are more important than a business deal. I know how much you love this project and your division, but we'll get there. You've already made an incredible amount of progress, and it's not like we need the money."

"I know," I answered, running a hand through my hair in frustration. I knew he was saying it was okay to put my needs first for a while. "But I'm multi-talented. I can handle more than one thing at a time."

"Cocky bastard," Trace replied good-naturedly. "Then get to it."

For the first time in two days, I felt the same sense of excitement I'd always experienced every time I had a challenge to tackle. "I'm on it," I answered firmly as I walked out of my brother's office.

Yesterday, I'd taken a day to feel sorry for myself.

Today, I was going on the offensive.

My assistant had seen me come in and I found my coffee already on my desk. I plucked a butterscotch candy from my dish, unwrapped it, and popped it into my mouth as I lifted my coffee.

After taking a gulp from my mug, I set it down and brought up my computer with a grin.

I didn't check my schedule.

I didn't start making calls.

For the first time since I'd become a partner at Walker, I had another priority, and it was one that couldn't wait.

CHAPTER 16

Paige

M *s. Rutledge:*
     I found a very large error in one of your con-
     tracts. I need you to report to me in my office as
soon as possible so the problem can be corrected.

Regards,

Sebastian Walker

*P.S. I can't seem to forget your breathless moans of pleasure or
the way you screamed out my name when you were in the throes of
your first orgasm. It gets my cock hard every time I think about it.*

I blinked at the computer screen, wondering if I'd had enough
coffee this morning. I'd just organized my desk to get to work,
and booted my computer up. Sebastian's message via the internal
message system was the first thing I saw on my screen.

I read the message three times, trying desperately to figure
out what mistake I'd made, and why he'd ended a formal message
with an erotic comment.

Did I really make a mistake?

No way! I was new at this job, and I checked and dou-
ble-checked my work to make sure everything was perfect.

It had taken me the rest of the weekend to come to grips with the fact that I'd never be intimate with Sebastian again. I was more than a little irritated that he seemed to be making light of what had been a life-changing night for me.

I chewed on my lip, and tapped my pen against my desk as I tried to figure out what he was up to. I wasn't really concerned about someone seeing the message. Nobody hacked into the private messages to and from either of the Walker brothers. If they did, they'd be fired. Almost everything else was subject to review.

I dropped the pen on the desk and replied:

Mr. Walker:

I don't make mistakes. Certainly you have the wrong attorney. My priority is always the best interests of your company. Please clarify what error you mistakenly think I've made.

Respectfully,

Paige Rutledge

P.S. I'll never forget Saturday night, either. You have a wicked tongue, Mr. Walker. Too bad I wasn't able to return the favor. I would have loved to try to suck on that monstrous cock of yours. I'm sure you taste...absolutely delicious.

"Take that," I said evilly as I pressed the button to send the message. If he wanted to play games, I could be just as down and dirty as he was.

I was fairly certain that there was no error made in any contract. He wanted to toy with me now that he'd fucked me.

It wasn't happening. I could give it right back to him.

I wasn't surprised to see another message blinking.

I pressed the button to view.

Paige,

You did make a mistake, and I need to see you up here now.

I stared at the quick message, wondering if he was serious.

I answered.

Sebastian,

This isn't funny. Don't mess with me.

A reply came back almost immediately.

Your gorgeous ass in my office now, or you're fired.

I rose from my chair fighting mad. There was no mistake, and he wasn't going to fire me just because he fucked me and couldn't take what he dished out.

I stomped out of my office and to the elevator, wondering if anyone could actually see the steam coming out of my ears. I hadn't been this pissed off in...well...I couldn't remember when it was. All I knew was that I was going to confront Sebastian Walker and tell him exactly what I thought of him using business to mock me personally.

There was nobody in the elevator as I stepped inside and pressed the button for the penthouse offices.

To think that I'd actually regretted leaving him after I'd thought about it Sunday morning, and wished I would have stayed. Regardless of how painful it might be for me later, Sebastian had shaken something up inside me, and I'd wished that I had relished every minute I could have had with him.

I owed him for making me realize that I wasn't dysfunctional. Well...maybe I *was* dysfunctional, but now at least I knew I wasn't *sexually* screwed up.

My new boots clicked on the tile floor as I exited the elevator, and I liked the powerful sound. I'd gone shopping yesterday to replace the things I'd borrowed from Sebastian's aunt, and I spontaneously decided to change my look. I certainly couldn't afford to shop in the same store where Sebastian had purchased my dress, but I'd been pretty good at staying trendy during my undergrad years on a budget. I *could* thank Sebastian for my sudden change in attitude, but I *wouldn't* because he had me pissed off. I had to admit that I felt more confident in the pretty sweater dress and heeled boots. My hair was still up, but I'd gone for a softer look, and some of the loose strands were brushing against my cheeks as I hightailed it to Sebastian's office. Hell, I'd even taken the time to put on more makeup.

"Can I help you?" a cautious female voice asked me as I passed her desk.

"I'm looking for Mr. Walker's office."

"Do you have an appointment?"

I smiled tightly at the middle-aged woman, trying to be polite. It wasn't her fault she worked for an asshole. "He's expecting me. I'm Paige Rutledge from legal."

She nodded her head toward a heavy wood door. "In there."

Determinedly, I moved to the door and turned the handle, pressing my weight against it. It swung open easily—too easily—and I had to turn around to close it.

I closed my eyes and leaned against the wood door. I knew the moment I saw him that I'd probably be unable to say what I wanted to say. I took a deep breath before I spoke. "I don't know what you think you're doing, but it's dirty and obnoxious. You can't just play with people's livelihoods. You know damn well I did nothing wrong. What in the hell is your problem?"

I listened to the silence for a moment before I heard an amused male voice speak. "I think I'm working, and I wasn't aware I *had* a problem."

My eyes flew open only to find that the man sitting behind the fancy desk in front of me was *not* Sebastian Walker.

"Oh, my God. I'm so sorry. I thought this was Mr. Walker's office." My cheeks flamed red, and I was so mortified that I wished I could just sink into the floor and end up back in my own, less spectacular office downstairs.

"I *am* Mr. Walker. Trace Walker. I take it you're looking for the dirty and obnoxious Sebastian?"

He grinned at me, and I felt like an even bigger idiot.

"Yes, sir," I answered, already envisioning Trace Walker firing me.

"Are you Paige?"

"Yes, sir," I admitted with a sigh, stepping forward to face the consequences.

He rose from his chair and walked around the desk, shocking me when he held out his hand. "Nice to meet you, Paige. I hope you're enjoying your job here at Walker."

"I was," I said glumly as I reached out and shook his hand. "I'm so sorry for what I said. I was angry—"

"Sebastian is my younger brother, and I'm sure it was provoked. Don't be sorry for standing up for yourself."

I blinked up at him, surprised he was actually letting me slide. "Thank you, Mr. Walker. I'll just get out of your office now." I wanted to get out of this room like my ass was on fire.

"Paige?" he called quietly.

I turned to face him again. "Yes."

"Whatever he might have done, Sebastian's a good man. He was always the kindest of the three of us, even as a kid. That hasn't changed since he grew up."

"I know. He lost track of who he really was," I answered automatically, then wished I could have bit my tongue.

Trace smiled, a genuine look of happiness on his face. "He knows now. He also knows exactly what he wants."

I was wondering where he was going with the conversation when he continued speaking.

"You're the first woman who has actually challenged him. Don't back off him, but give him a break if you can."

"He's annoying," I mumbled. "He threatened to fire me if I didn't get to his office immediately."

Trace nodded his head toward his left. "He's right next door. And yes, he can be obnoxious, but it's all a cover. I think you already know exactly who he is."

I nodded, trying to work out what was happening with Sebastian's brother. "I'm not sure I do know. His message—"

"Was no doubt a ploy to get you up here," Trace finished. "He's crazy about you."

I opened my mouth, then closed it again. "I think you misunderstand our relationship."

Trace leaned a hip against his desk and crossed his arms. "I don't think I do. I just went through the same thing a year ago with my wife."

"What is she like?" I asked curiously, wondering what kind of woman could tame one of the Walker brothers.

He smiled broader. "Strong, stubborn, beautiful, and sassy as hell. But she has an enormous heart, big enough to accept me with all of my faults. But her life wasn't easy. She's a survivor. Sound familiar?"

"You know me? I don't think we've ever met."

"I know you through Sebastian."

"Oh." I couldn't think of anything else to say. I couldn't imagine Sebastian talking about me to his brother. "Your wife sounds lovely," I answered politely.

"She is," he acknowledged.

I heard the door open behind me before I could respond.

"What in the hell are you doing? I said *my* office," Sebastian said irritably.

I turned around to face him. "I got the wrong Walker. How would I know where your office is? I've never even been on this floor."

"Ask," he suggested.

"I did. I still ended up here," I told him patiently.

I watched as Sebastian glared at his older brother, who was now openly chuckling.

Sebastian moved forward and gripped my upper arm. "Let's go."

"Don't kill each other," I heard Trace Walker remark as Sebastian dragged me out of his brother's office and into his own.

As Sebastian closed the door, I shrugged off his hold on my arm. "Now I can tell *you* instead of your brother: stop messing with my livelihood."

He turned around with a furious glare. "Why? You aren't doing what you want to do anyway. You said business law wasn't your first choice. Why are you here?"

His comment hit its mark, but I tried not to show it. I ignored his provocation. "Just show me the error so I can be on my way."

"I can just tell you. It was actually a verbal contract."

"Fine. Tell me."

"I asked you to stay for a month, and you agreed. Then for some unknown reason, you decided to leave before I woke up in the morning. One month. Then we say goodbye. Why in the hell did you go, Paige?"

He was angry, but I could hear the desperation in his voice. "I had to. And I never really agreed to your verbal contract. You just assumed I did."

"That's why you called me up here? To suggest that I broke a sex contract?"

"You did," he confirmed, his nostrils flaring and the muscle in his jaw contracting. "God dammit, Paige. Do you know how fucking worried I was when I woke up and you were gone?" He stepped forward and grabbed me by the shoulders, shaking me lightly. "Do you?"

I stared at him with a blank expression before I answered. "I left a note."

I was honest. I didn't actually know what it felt like for somebody to worry about me. I hadn't since I lost my parents. The only one who cared was Kenzie, and I didn't have her close to me anymore.

"I left because I was scared," I told him anxiously.

"Why?"

"Because I knew we couldn't be together again. If we were, it would break me." I might as well admit it. "I never meant to care about you this much, I never thought I'd feel what I'm feeling right now." I was shouting now, but I didn't care. "I'm falling in love with you, and I didn't know what else to do."

Mortified that I'd actually said those words aloud, I turned around and fled.

CHAPTER 17

Sebastian

I lost valuable time standing in my office like an idiot, trying to wrap my head around the fact that Paige had feelings for me.

Me.

The former player.

She's not falling for the player, dammit. Paige is beginning to care about...me.

"Fuck!" I growled aloud, then turned and followed her, determined not to let her run away.

I knew how tempting that instinct could be. But it wasn't happening.

Taking the stairs to save time, I was banking on the fact that it was the beginning of a workday, and there was no way she'd leave the building. She was too damn conscientious.

I took the stairs two at a time, unwilling to wait for an elevator. When I reached the floor beneath my office, I burst into the open area near the elevators and sprinted to Paige's office.

I stopped short as I heard the heartbreaking sobs as I stood at the door.

I felt like a jerk because hearing her emotional turmoil in the form of distress actually made me feel hopeful. But after that initial reaction, I desperately wanted her to stop. Yeah, I was happy because she hadn't dumped me because she didn't care about me. She'd kicked me to the curb because she was fucking terrified.

My anger fled just as quickly as it had appeared, and I turned the handle to let myself in, but it was locked.

"Paige," I howled, not giving a shit about the other people in her office. "Open the damn door." I tried to look through the glass windows, but the blinds were closed.

The muffled noises from inside her office ceased, and the entire department went deadly quiet until I heard her modulated request. "Go away. You're making a scene."

I grinned, knowing she'd moved up to the door so only I could hear her.

"Either open the door or I'll make more than a scene. It will be a major production."

I waited, knowing she was probably battling with herself, trying to decide which was worse: me making a ruckus, or facing me.

When I heard the lock click, I knew she didn't want to look unprofessional and become a subject of gossip in the office.

Good choice.

"I said everything I have to say," she said coolly as she opened the door, blocking the entrance with her body.

Finding it slightly amusing that she thought standing in the front of the door would stop me from coming in, I curled one arm around her waist, closing the door and twirling her out of the way at the same time. I then clicked the lock, not wanting to be disturbed.

I nearly groaned as her delectable body slid slowly down mine until her booted feet touched the floor.

She struggled out of my grip and I let her go, wondering if she was feeling like an animal trapped in its own den. I didn't want that, but dammit, I was going to make her listen to me.

"Well, I haven't said all that I have to say," I replied, striding forward to sit on the edge of her desk. "I want to know why you're so afraid of anybody caring about you. You *did* scare the shit out of me yesterday morning."

She turned her back to me. "I already told you why."

I had to cross my arms over my chest to stop myself from reaching for her. "Tell me again. Because to my way of thinking, caring about somebody isn't a bad thing."

"It is when you know those feelings will never be returned," she said in a tremulous voice. "Sebastian, I can't do this. My work is my life."

I ran a hand through my hair in frustration. "Mine, too. And that's fucked up," I answered gruffly. "Because I'm falling in love with you, too, Paige. Hell, I'm probably already splattered on the cement at your feet."

She whirled around to face me, the expression on her face startled. "Y-You can't. W-We can't," she stammered.

I stood up again and grasped her shoulders. "See, now that's the thing...we actually can—very easily. Why can't *we* just... happen? Why does it have to be so fucking difficult? You let me show you how much I care, and you stop running away from anything that scares you."

"I'm not used to it," she admitted breathlessly, her beautiful blue eyes staring up at me with apprehension in their depths.

"Then get used to it," I insisted. There was no way I was giving her up now.

Paige Rutledge belonged with me. I didn't give a damn about the fact that she worked for my company. All I knew was that she'd worked her ass off and had been through hell. *Dammit!* It screwed with my head that she hadn't had somebody who gave a shit about what happened to her.

"Not a good idea," she answered shakily.

"What?"

"You and me. We have to stop this now."

"Why in the hell are you running away?" I questioned angrily. "It's not like I didn't just tell you that I feel the same way you do. And I'm not giving up."

"You're not in my position," she explained, irritated. "You're the head of the company. I work for that company, and I'm just getting a foothold here. One wrong move and I'll screw myself. I don't have the luxury of taking chances."

She was right, and I wasn't sure how to convince her that no matter what happened, I'd never do anything to hurt her. "Write a contract. If you leave Walker for any reason within the next year, you get two million dollars in severance pay and a good reference. I'll sign it. I know you know how to make it an iron clad contract that I can never get out of."

I watched as she opened and closed her mouth several times, but never said a word. Finally, she replied, "No. That would be crazy."

I shrugged. Honestly, I didn't care if it was lunacy. "I want you to be able to trust that I won't screw with your career, or leave you in a bad situation, no matter what happens. Be with me. Spend time with me. Let's face it, neither one of us are exactly normal. We spend almost every waking hour working. We have no fucking balance in our lives."

"But I want to advance—"

"And I want to light up the world with renewable energy," I interrupted. "But I'll get there, and you'll advance in your career, but we can do those things without making ourselves crazy. Take a chance, Paige. You'll have a contract that will cover you in every possible way. There's no reason not to try anymore."

I watched as confusion flooded her beautiful face before she said, "Sebastian, doing a contract like that is nuts. You'd have no way out if I quit tomorrow."

"Are you planning on leaving?"

"No."

"Then there are no issues."

"Most people would just quit," she observed. "Two million is a big incentive. A new attorney doesn't make that much in a decade."

"Then you can quit and just take the money."

"Why are you doing this?" she asked huskily, her voice trembling with vulnerability.

"Because even if you don't trust me, I trust you," I answered with raw honesty. "I don't think you'd leave within that year unless you really had to. You're too damn honorable."

"You can't know that."

"I'm a betting man. I'm willing to take that chance on you."

She just kept staring at me, and I was starting to sweat. I needed her to say 'yes' and I needed it right fucking now. But I waited. Paige had dealt with things a woman should never have to deal with in a lifetime. Her agreeing to give us a chance would still be a leap of faith. A guy with my history was a risk, and the last emotional gamble a woman like her would want to take on.

"We need to set ground rules," she instructed. "We're dating, trying each other out. It can't affect my work."

"Okay. But we leave work by five, unless there are extenuating circumstances."

She nodded slowly. "Are we going to keep having sex?"

"Oh, hell yeah," I answered in a graveled voice. "A lot."

She pretended to consider my answer before she said, "I think I can live with that."

I wrapped my arms around her waist. "Good. Because I can't live without it," I rumbled before I couldn't stop myself from sealing the deal with the kiss I'd been waiting to lay on her since I'd woken up and found her gone.

I knew the embrace was rough and carnal, but my relief of knowing that she wasn't going to slip away coursed through my body, and territorial instincts consumed me.

I needed her.

And I knew that she needed me.

Hell, even if she didn't, she was going to get me anyway. I'd been under Paige's spell almost since the moment I'd met her.

I was eventually able to pull my mouth from hers so we could both breathe, but it wasn't enough. Lifting her up by the ass, I turned and planted her on the desk.

"Sebastian—"

I kissed her again, cutting off her words. I didn't want to hear about how we couldn't fuck at work, and I knew that was what she was going to say. But she was breathing as hard as I was, and as I yanked up her dress and discovered that all she was wearing was a pair of delicate panties and thigh-high stockings, I damn near lost it.

I passed my fingers lightly over the silky strip of fabric between her thighs, my heart pounding as I felt how wet that garment was.

Yanking my lips from her, I groaned. "Christ, you're so wet, baby."

I delved under the elastic and stroked her clit.

"Oh, God," she said in a breathy voice that made me crazy.

I reveled in the fact that I could make her feel good. "Let me, Paige," I demanded.

"We're working," she protested weakly as she tangled her hands in my hair.

I nibbled at the sensitive skin of her neck, and my reply was muffled. "We work plenty of overtime, and I own the desk I'm going to fuck you on right now."

"Mr. Hurst—"

"Is conveniently in a meeting with Trace right now," I growled as I reached down to pull the dress over her head, then lowered her upper body down on the desk.

"This is dangerous," she panted, her cheeks flushed with passion.

Christ! She looked so damn beautiful that I felt like I'd been sucker punched in the gut. It wasn't just the gorgeous image of her spread out and so damn aroused on her desk, but the fact that she was taking a chance. A big one. On *me.*

I was so damn ready to get myself inside her that I tore the fragile panties from her body and slipped them into my pocket.

I flipped the front clasp on her bra with clumsy fingers, then cupped her beautiful breasts, stroking the hardened nipples with my thumbs.

Mine!

I stroked my palms over her silken skin, my eyes focused on an image that I knew would be engraved on my memory for a lifetime.

Paige's beautiful body spread out on her desk, waiting for me to fuck her.

"Sebastian," she whimpered in a needy voice.

Her fire belonged to me, and it was me she was counting on to sate her.

I grasped her hands and placed them over her breasts. "Do what feels good."

As I moved my fingers up her thighs, then let them plunge into her moist heat, I watched her eyes close as she pleasured her breasts, then wished I hadn't asked her to do that.

The sight was too damn erotic.

"You're so beautiful, Paige," I said hoarsely as I stroked her clit with one hand and fumbled with my pants and fly with the other.

"Oh, God. That feels so good," she whispered, her head moving back and forth on the desk as she pinched and stroked her nipples.

It was about to get a whole lot better for both of us. I liberated my cock, resisting the urge to go down on her to wring every climax from her that I could. It was the wrong place at the wrong time. There were people working in nearby offices and cubicles. The last thing I wanted to do was embarrass her. There would be time for everything else later.

Right now, I just fucking needed to claim her.

"Fuck me, Sebastian," she pleaded softly.

"Done," I grunted, removing my fingers from her pussy and replacing them with my rock-hard erection.

She gasped as I buried myself to the balls inside her fiery, wet sheath.

Gritting my teeth to stay still, I asked, "Did I hurt you?"

"No. No. Please. More."

I grasped her hips, relieved, and started a punishing rhythm that I knew was going to make us both satisfied.

There was very little noise except our harsh breathing and the slapping of flesh as I fucked her as passionately as I needed… as we both desperately wanted.

Watching her aroused face, and her rough stimulation of her breasts drove me nearly insane. Her booted legs wrapped around my waist, urging me faster and faster.

"Fuck!" I cursed as I felt my orgasm coming on in record time.

Paige was panting, and biting her lip to keep from moaning aloud, a sight that almost made her as sexy as when she was screaming my name.

In desperation, I moved one hand from her ass and gave her the strong stroking pressure she needed on the tiny bundle of nerves just above where our bodies were joined. She struggled even harder not to cry out, but a low moan escaped her lips.

"Come for me, Paige. I can't hold out much longer." My pace on her clit increased.

Relief flooded through me as I felt her thighs trembling, and her channel start to clamp down on my cock.

"Feels so good. You feel so good," she said almost incoherently.

I shot off as she massaged my cock with her spasms, and I groaned as I released myself inside her as she struggled not to scream.

I plunged inside her with one last deep stroke, put a hand under her back and sat her up, quickly covering her mouth with mine as I absorbed the sounds of her climax, and reveling in my own.

I held her quivering body against me long after we'd both been satisfied, unable to let her go.

Thank fuck she's mine!

A shudder of satisfaction ran through my body, a primitive reaction that I didn't understand because I'd never experienced it before. But I didn't question my possessive instincts. When it came Paige, they just...existed.

Eventually, we separated and silently put ourselves back together in the small attached bathroom she had in her office.

I stood behind her, straightening my tie in the mirror as she fixed her hair.

"I can't believe I just fucked a man on my office desk," she said weakly.

"Not just any man, baby. You fucked me," I said arrogantly, satisfied that my tie was okay.

"The boss," she groaned. "The damn owner of Walker."

"Not him," I told her as I turned her around. "Me. Sebastian."

There was a distinct difference between fucking the boss and fucking a guy you cared about.

She wrapped her hands around my neck. "I wouldn't have done it if it wasn't you," she said quietly, her ocean-blue eyes looked at me openly. "*Sebastian* is irresistible to me for some reason."

My heartrate kicked up as I stared down at her, not giving a shit about why she cared about me. I was just damn grateful that she did.

I kissed her on the forehead so I didn't mess up the light coat of lipstick she'd just applied, then rested my forehead against hers. "Damn good thing, because you drive me to the edge of insanity, sweetheart." I hesitated before asking, "Dinner tonight?"

I pulled my head back to look at her. There was a noticeably mischievous look in her eyes as she answered, "Why, yes. I think I'd love to join you for dinner. But I have a problem."

I frowned. "What?"

"I seem to have lost my panties, and this sweater dress clings. If I bend the wrong way, anybody within seeing distance will be staring at my butt crack."

I didn't like the thought of anybody looking at my woman's ass. "I'll fix it."

"Do you keep a large supply of women's underwear handy?" she asked in a teasing tone.

"Trust me," I requested in an equally joking voice.

"Okay," she said simply. "Now I have to get back to work."

We exited the tiny bathroom, and I walked toward the door. "You have a contract to write. An order coming directly from the top," I reminded her.

"I'll put the job on my list," she answered lightly.

"Make it a priority," I insisted as I unlocked the door and turned to look at her.

"See you at five," she said in a husky voice.

"I'll be here," I vowed.

I'd make it to her office to pick her up. If not, then I'd have to be dead.

This was a new start for both of us, and I sensed in my gut that it was going to be good.

I broke eye contact with her, knowing if I didn't, I was never going to leave her office without fucking her again.

I closed the door quietly behind me, trying not to draw attention to myself, then headed for the elevator with a grin on my face.

CHAPTER 18

Paige

*L*ater that day, I was still smiling as I finished my last contract.

I'd done a lot of thinking off and on all afternoon, and I knew Sebastian was right. I was running, moving away from anything emotionally dangerous to cocoon myself from ever getting hurt.

If I was ever going to break out of the shell of protection I'd wrapped myself in, the man to shatter it was going to be Sebastian.

I wish I could say I hadn't been a coward for so many years, using my ambitions to distance me from having any kind of personal life. Maybe before Sebastian, it hadn't mattered. There had never been anyone I'd wanted to be with, but my life was changing. And so was I.

The rap on my office door startled me, and I instinctively looked up at the clock. It was only four.

"Come in," I called out, assuming it was a co-worker or my boss.

"Delivery for Ms. Paige Rutledge."

The visitor stepped into the office and laid a wrapped box on the desk in front of me, and I scrambled in the desk drawer, desperately seeking a tip for the delivery. When I found it, I tried to hand the bills to the young guy who'd brought me the package.

He waved it away. "I work for the Walkers, ma'am," he said politely. "I don't do tips."

He turned and walked out of the office, and I stuffed the money back in my purse.

I knew without a doubt that the package was from Sebastian, especially if the messenger was on a Walker salary.

Lifting the lightweight box, I opened it carefully, pushed back the liberal amount of tissue paper on the top, then gaped at the items inside.

I reached out a tentative finger to touch the delicate silk and lace, dazzled by the lingerie, but slightly dismayed. The panties were from the most expensive designers in the country, and it was a bit frightening to wear a pair of underwear that probably cost more than my car payment.

Rummaging through the tissue paper, I finally found a note:

Paige,

I didn't want you to be walking around town with no under-wear. Nobody sees your ass but me. The other item is something I noticed that you seem to miss.

S.

I laughed because it was a thoughtful gift, but not exactly without self-interest. Did he think my rounded butt would get much attention? He obviously thought so, and I couldn't help but smile.

I noticed a small box tucked beside the panties and opened it curiously. What was inside stunned me so much that I was motionless and silent.

My mouth hung open for an undetermined amount of time while I stared at the gorgeous watch made up of rose gold, the timepiece encrusted with diamonds. I instantly adored it, and

I finally gently lifted the box and removed the delicate watch, cringing as I noticed it was a very exclusive jewelry company.

It fit perfectly, and it felt so good to have a watch back on my wrist. It was absolutely stunning, but I knew I couldn't accept a gift that expensive.

I finally picked out a pretty pair of panties, hesitating to even put them on. The lacework and bows were exquisite, but I couldn't imagine my ass in the seductive underwear.

"He could have just gone to Walmart," I grumbled to myself. But I knew Sebastian was trying to please me, and I hadn't had that kind of attention in a long time. The things he'd bought were probably normal for his status, but they were far from ordinary for me.

Before I could change my mind, I carefully put my feet into the underwear, careful not to snag them on the heels of my boots. Once I'd pulled them up, I sighed. Maybe I couldn't understand paying a fortune for panties, but they felt divine.

I actually felt…sexy.

Wrapping up the rest of the collection of panties in the tissue paper again, I placed them carefully back into the box, along with the watch case, and closed the lid. I was fairly certain that the store wouldn't do returns on panties, even though I'd never worn the rest of them. But the watch had to go back.

I was just contemplating what to do when my phone rang.

"Paige Rutledge," I murmured professionally into the mouthpiece of the phone.

"Hi, Paige. I'm sorry to bother you at work. This is Eva Walker."

Trace's wife? Why was she calling me?

Assuming she was calling about work, I answered, "What can I do for you?"

"You could attend a dinner I'm doing Thursday night at our place. I heard you were on friendly terms with Sebastian, and he doesn't have a date. I need an ally if I'm going to get through Thanksgiving with the Walker brothers. I feel outnumbered, so Trace asked me to ask you."

I was taken aback by the invitation, and I'd actually forgotten that Thanksgiving was coming. "Um...thanks..." *Oh, shit!* What should I say?

"I'd love to meet you in person. I want to see the woman who brought Sebastian to his knees," Eva said with a delighted laugh.

"I haven't...I don't...Oh, hell, we just decided to give each other a trial period. We aren't really together."

Eva was quiet for a minute before she replied, "Sebastian said that?"

"Yes."

"He's so lying. He's crazy about you."

"It's what he asked for," I countered.

"What a dope," she replied, her voice filled with affection, even though she was insulting her brother-in-law. "Trace said Sebastian is done for since he met you."

"I'm done for, too," I confessed, completely giving up on denying the truth. Eva sounded so damn nice that I wanted to be honest with her.

"Good. Then you won't mind coming to dinner with your future husband."

"He's not...He won't..." *Shit!* I was starting to sound like an idiot.

"He will," Eva said confidently. "In the meantime, please join us. Trace told me you're new and moved from the East Coast. Nobody should be alone on Thanksgiving."

I could tell her I'd been alone plenty at the holidays for years, but I didn't want to sound like a major loser. "That's very kind of you," I said honestly. Nobody had ever given a damn whether I spent the holidays by myself, except Kenzie.

"Then you'll come?"

Honestly, when the big boss's wife asks you to dinner, you go. "Of course. What can I bring?"

We chatted for a while, Eva refusing to let me bring a thing except myself. I'd have to find some wine, and bring it anyway.

There was no way I was going to her house and not bring something with me.

We settled on a time, an hour before the dinner would be ready since she didn't want anyone in her kitchen, and hung up.

I sighed as I put the receiver back on the cradle. Eva seemed very nice, but the dinner was bound to be awkward. I'd never met her or anybody else she'd probably invite except Sebastian. And yeah, there was that short, embarrassing meeting I'd had with Trace Walker.

"Paige!" The booming voice pulled me back to reality.

I turned my head and saw Sebastian leaning against the frame of the open door.

"I'm sorry. I was lost in thought," I explained.

"About what? I called your name three times and you didn't answer." He walked in and closed the door. "Everything okay?"

"Yeah. Fine. Except your sister-in-law just called and invited me to dinner on Thursday."

"What did you tell her?"

"I said I'd go, of course. I was kind of in a difficult position."

He nodded as he sat on the edge of my desk. "I was going to ask you to go myself, but I was a little...distracted this morning."

"I won't know anybody there except you."

"You've met Trace."

I smiled at him sheepishly. "Yeah, well, that was fairly mortifying. I was telling him off because I thought I was in your office."

Sebastian's lips turned up in that mischievous grin that I loved so much, then confirmed, "I know. He told me. He likes you. Says you have spunk." He paused before adding, "Dane will be there, too. You haven't met him, but he's quiet and I doubt you'll find him intimidating."

"He's coming here? I know Kenzie would love to meet him. She's a major fan of his artwork."

"He'll be there. He doesn't get out much in public, but he'll make the family holidays."

"Nobody else?" I asked curiously.

"Nope. Aunt Aileen asked us to come to her resort for the holidays, but we were afraid Dane might bail on us if we didn't keep it small, so we passed this year."

I started shutting down my computer as I said, "Okay. I might be able to handle that."

Sebastian sat in the chair in front of my desk. "You're not going to cancel at the last minute, are you?"

I looked up for a moment, and our eyes met knowingly. "I'd like to get conveniently ill, but no. I'm going. It was kind of Eva to invite me, and I've stopped running away from situations that might be uncomfortable at first."

Sebastian lifted a brow. "Have you?"

I shrugged. "I'm going to try. I'm all grown up, and I don't need those defenses quite as much as I did several years ago. Maybe they helped back then, but I want to be me again, Sebastian. I used to know how to live in the moment, how to have fun and enjoy nice people. I wasn't tense every waking hour worrying about sticking to a life plan."

He searched my face before replying. "Making plans and having goals isn't always a bad thing. They only suck when they take priority over everything and everyone else."

"Exactly," I said, tearing my eyes from his face as I gathered up my purse and stood. "Were the panties and the watch your spontaneous deed for the day?" Obviously he'd stopped thinking about work long enough to order them.

He rose from his chair. "One of several things, actually. Were they okay?"

"The underwear were expensive," I chastised him. "I may not own any, but I recognize the brands. And they're beautiful. Thank you."

"Don't thank me. I was the one who created your underwear dilemma in the first place," he joked in a low, teasing baritone.

"I'm not going to argue about that." My body let out a little involuntary shudder as I remembered that moment when he'd ripped my inexpensive lingerie in a moment of abandon passion before I added, "Sebastian, I can't accept the watch." I held up my wrist. "It's gorgeous, and I did lose my watch during my move, but it's too pricey. My old watch wasn't expensive."

He shrugged. "It's just a small gift. You're keeping it. It looks good on you."

I sighed. "A small gift for you. A big gift for me."

"Sorry. It was on sale. I can't return it."

"Since when do you buy sale items?" I questioned skeptically. I knew damn well he could return it if he chose to do so.

"Since today," he answered with a playful smile.

"I call bullshit."

"Can't you just say thanks without an argument? I wanted you to have it. Call it a graduation gift."

I burst out laughing because I couldn't help myself. "You didn't even know me when I graduated."

"See how much I missed and need to make up for?" he answered impishly.

God, this man could make me crazy. "Just this once," I agreed. "As long as you let me do something for you."

"You can give me the contract," he suggested.

"Sorry," I answered, being deliberately contrary. "I was much too busy today. You'll have to think up something else."

In truth, there was no way I was ever going to write up that agreement. I cared too much about him to make him put his ass on the line to trust him. I was either going to change...or I wasn't. My choice was to start being me again, trust the guy I cared about.

"My choices would be entirely X-rated," he warned.

I'd never inspired any kind of unbridled passion in any guy, and the way Sebastian looked at me, touched me, was still so unbelievable to me.

"What are you thinking?" he asked.

"About this morning when you tore those panties," I answered bluntly.

He groaned as he wrapped his arms around me. "Fuck. Don't remind me or I'll bend you over your desk and do it again."

"Not with these panties you won't," I told him firmly, but I was smiling as I rested my hands on his broad, muscular shoulders.

"Don't count on it," he warned ominously, right before he kissed me.

It started as a leisurely kiss, an embrace of exploration that quickly turned carnal and needy. I moaned against his lips, and he pulled his mouth from mine.

"Jesus! I can't touch you without wanting to bury my dick inside you," he growled, kissing my forehead before he stepped back.

I knew what he meant. Sebastian and I were like kindling and a match. Put us together and all we wanted to do was burn.

"Can you feed me first?" I asked shakily.

"No lunch?" he asked in a disapproving voice.

I shrugged. "I was trying to make sure I put in a lot of work. I have a dinner date with the sexiest, smartest, sweetest man on earth. I didn't want to miss a moment of it."

Sebastian took my coat from the hanger by the door and held it out for me as he said in a hungry, throaty tone, "He would have waited for you, no matter how long it took. You could have eaten lunch."

My heart skittered at the heat and sincerity in his voice. "I haven't had a date in a very long time."

"Me either. But we're going to make up for that." He nuzzled against my upswept hair. "I just wish you didn't smell so damn good."

"I'll change shampoos," I told him, pretty certain my eyes were shining with mirth as I turned around to face him.

"No," he said hastily. "Don't. I'm a damn masochist, but I love the way your smell fucking tortures me. Besides, it wouldn't matter. You'll always smell the same to me."

"Like cherry blossoms?" I asked curiously.

"No. Like you're fucking mine," he answered hoarsely and held out his hand.

The thought that we shouldn't be obvious that we were more than friends when I was still at Walker with him flitted through my mind, but I discarded it just as quickly.

It was my time.

I was done working.

And I adored the way Sebastian treated me with affection.

I really was done running away from my emotions. And I wanted to feel a connection with him, too.

I smiled and took his hand, ignoring the speculative glances we got since most people were in the process of leaving for the day.

In the short period of time that it took for us to get out of the building, I realized I had my own possessive instincts.

I focused on the immense satisfaction of letting everybody know that Sebastian was taken…at least for now.

CHAPTER 19

Paige

"I think I should wear something else," I told Sebastian nervously as I fiddled with the blue sweater I was wearing. "It doesn't feel right to be wearing jeans to the boss's house."

I'd tried to dress the outfit up with a silver belt, my boots, and extra makeup. But I still felt underdressed.

"You look beautiful," Sebastian drawled from his position on his massive bed, his back against the headboard. "I told you, we don't dress up for the holidays. We spend our days in suits and office attire. When we aren't working and with family, we want to be comfortable."

I glanced at him through the mirror, thinking Sebastian would look gorgeous in anything...or nothing. He was currently dressed in a tan fisherman's sweater and a pair of dark jeans, a casual outfit that made him look as hot as he appeared in one of his custom power suits. Maybe more so because he looked so carefree and happy.

Sebastian and I had spent almost every moment of our free time the last several days in each other's company, and I cherished every moment. It wasn't that what we were doing was all that exciting, but I'd discovered that the time I spent with him was a few of the happiest days I could remember.

Every day I looked forward to being with him.

And every night was an adventure. *Okay. Yes.* Those experiences usually required us both being naked. But even having dinner together, talking about our days was fun when I was with him. We shared pretty much the same interests when it came to television and movies, and we both loved the same food.

I'd discovered why Sebastian's delicious scent always seemed to include a hint of butterscotch. Because he'd stopped smoking weed and cigarettes, he kept a bowl of candies on his desk at all times, gourmet butterscotch hard candy that he'd gotten me practically addicted to.

I turned around and looked over my shoulder to review my rear end. "I have to stop eating those candies. I can see them on my ass," I grumbled.

"I'd be happy to lick them off for you," Sebastian answered with an evil grin.

I glared at him, trying to keep a straight face when I wanted to smile. "My jeans are too tight."

"They aren't," he contradicted. "And your ass is perfect. I have fantasies about it."

"Wicked fantasies?" I asked hopefully.

He quirked his brow. "Very. Want me to tell you about them?"

"No!" I exclaimed. "We'll end up late for dinner."

I was already nervous enough about having dinner with his family. I didn't want to be rude by being late.

Sebastian rose from the bed like a predator on the prowl. "Trace would understand," he said persuasively as he wrapped his muscular arms around my waist.

He was insatiable, and I loved it, but I wasn't giving in. "We just got out of bed."

We'd spent the entire morning lazing around naked, one passionate session right after the one before.

"Yeah. And I resent it," Sebastian answered, his voice amused.

"You do not." I pushed him away firmly. "You haven't seen Dane for a long time, and you already told me Eva's an incredible chef."

"I miss Dane," he answered thoughtfully.

"I'm sure you do," I said, giving him a sympathetic glance.

Sebastian had explained that Dane had been badly scarred in the plane crash which had taken away his father and his stepmother. So I knew why he was self-conscious about being in public.

"Ready?" he asked, pocketing his keys and his wallet.

"As ready as I'll ever be." I wasn't going to get beautiful and thin before I got to Trace's house, so I'd have to deal with how I looked.

"Don't be nervous. You'll like Trace and Eva, and Dane is a nice guy."

I shot him a smile I wasn't really feeling. It wasn't that I didn't want to be with his family. I wanted them to like me. "I'm just a little nervous. It's a little intimidating to be eating Thanksgiving dinner with a bunch of powerful people."

"We're human," Sebastian said as he took my hand to lead me downstairs. "We celebrate Thanksgiving just like everybody else."

I doubted that. Sebastian was like no guy I'd ever known, but in a good way. Since we hadn't been able to have sex every minute we were together, we'd gotten to know each other very well over the last few days. I'd come home with him every night, and I'd started leaving clothing and personal items at his house. I couldn't say I hadn't gotten lost a time or two in the massive residence, but I was gradually getting comfortable with his wealth and his home.

"I know," I agreed as he led me down the stairs.

I understood that Sebastian wasn't back at Walker for the money he could make. His love for alternative energy was clear in everything he did. He enjoyed his job, and he was passionate about solar technology. He was teaching me more and more about the science, and I was an enthusiastic listener.

I also was aware that Trace carried on his father's company to keep his legacy going.

Dane pursued his art.

None of the Walkers were like any of the rich guys I'd known, and I knew I couldn't put them all in the same mold.

I thought for a moment as Sebastian stopped near the kitchen to get the fruit salad and wine I'd gotten for Eva. Finally, I confessed, "Even if you weren't rich, I'd still be nervous."

He grabbed the bag from the fridge, sitting it on the counter while we both got into our coats. "Why?" he asked curiously.

"Because this is your family," I answered simply. "I want them to like me."

"Sweetheart, they'll love you."

I shrugged. "I hope so."

"Trust me," he said solemnly.

"I do."

He hauled me out the garage door, then settled me into the car before getting into the driver's seat.

After he buckled up, he reached into the console between the bucket seats and pulled out a handful of those lethal, butt-widening butterscotch sweets.

"Candy?" he offered mischievously, holding out his hand with the offering.

I was a stress eater, and Sebastian knew it. I glared at him, but snatched a few of the tempting, rich treats from his hand, then watched as he took one, unwrapped it, then popped it into his mouth.

"If I pop out of these jeans, it's all your fault," I grumbled as I unwrapped a butterscotch, the smell making my mouth water as it went from my hand to my mouth. As the taste exploded on my tongue, I asked curiously, "Where did you get these? They're addictive." I'd had plenty of this type of candy, but none had ever been this good.

He opened the garage door as he answered. "Imported. My assistant started me on them. I emptied the candy dish in the office in one day. Now I always have a full bowl every morning."

I rolled my eyes. Of course he could eat a pound of candy a day and still have a perfectly sculpted body. "I'd be even chubbier than I am now."

"You're fucking perfect," Sebastian answered as he maneuvered onto the street.

I both loved and hated it when he said things like that. It was disarming. "You know I'm not." After all, he was feeling up my body on a nightly basis.

"To me you are," he answered simply.

And...what in the hell could I say to that? Sebastian accepted me exactly the way I was, Italian curvy figure and all. "Thank you," I answered softly, meaning so much more than just the words.

"I'm not sure why you're worried. We work out every single night," he answered in a naughty tone that sent shivers of desire up my spine.

I batted his arm playfully. "Pervert."

"Guilty," he said. "I'm horny every single moment you're with me."

I smiled as I crunched on the last of my butterscotch, totally unable to worry about how I looked when Sebastian acted like I was the most gorgeous woman on the planet.

"No wonder I adore you," I teased.

"I hope you still do by the end of today," he mumbled in a low, slightly-worried voice.

"I thought you said everything would be fine."

"I hope it will be," he answered mysteriously.

"What happened to your certainty that your family would love me?"

"Oh, they will," he said confidently.

"Then what are you worried about?" His cryptic comments were starting to make me nervous.

"Paige, I..." his voice trailed off, his statement unfinished.

"What?" I looked at his profile, trying to figure out what was bothering him.

He shook his head. "Nothing. You'll find out soon enough."

"Sebastian, you're worrying me," I warned him.

"Don't," he requested as he took my hand in his. "Everything will be fine."

I savored the closeness as he entwined our fingers. I couldn't see his eyes, so it was hard to understand if he was truly concerned about something. "Okay. I trust you."

He groaned. "That's why I'm a little concerned."

"Why?"

"I sort of invited a few extra guests."

"I thought it was just family."

Trace and Sebastian lived within a few miles of each other, so we were already pulling into the parking lot of the high-rise building where Sebastian had said Trace had the penthouse.

"Technically, it is just family," he answered vaguely.

"Tell me who else is coming. I hate surprises."

"I know," he answered, his voice sounding pained as he parked his vehicle and hopped out without answering the question.

He moved quickly, helping me out of the car, locking it up, then entwining our fingers again as we walked into the building and into the elevator that led to Trace's penthouse.

I was tense, sensing Sebastian was hiding something. As the elevator went up, I started to feel extremely uneasy. "You invited your extended family? Am I going to get overwhelmed by billionaires?"

"No." He pinned me against the elevator wall, a hand planted on each side of my body so I couldn't escape. "Paige, I love you," he said huskily, his eyes locking with mine. "Remember that."

I fell into his dark gaze, my body trembling, my heart about to beat right out of my chest as I grasped the edges of the black jacket he was wearing. "What?"

He'd never said those words before, but as I searched his expression, I knew that he meant them.

"I fucking love you," he rasped. "I think I have almost since the moment I met you. Maybe it's not rational to believe in love-at-first-sight, but it was more than just the fact that I wanted to fuck you. I sensed you, and I was drawn to you like an obsession that would never go away. It's just gotten stronger every day. I want you to be happy."

Tears began to leak from my eyes, and my emotions were out of control.

I pulled his head down and kissed him, trying to convey how much his words meant to me without words. Because honestly, words couldn't express how much Sebastian meant to me.

He kissed me back with a desperation that took my breath away, and we both emerged panting as the elevator came to a stop.

He rested his forehead against mine as he said, "Everything amazing happens in an elevator for us."

I wanted to tell him that I loved him, too. That his support and unconditional love meant everything to me.

But I didn't have the chance as we breathlessly exited the lift, and noticed the door to what had to be Trace's penthouse was already open.

I stopped in my tracks, stunned as I realized exactly who else Sebastian had invited to Thanksgiving dinner, as they waited right outside the door.

Confused, I shook my head in denial. "Mom? Dad?"

My heart shattered into pieces as I confronted the two people that I'd loved the most in the world; wonderful parents who I thought I'd have for a lifetime, but who eventually left me to face the darkness alone.

Sebastian squeezed my hand, keeping a firm grip on me. I knew he was probably afraid I'd run. But my days of hiding were over.

I didn't turn around and leave.

Instead, I felt the tears start to flow down my face like a warm river as I finally faced the excruciating pain of what I'd lost.

CHAPTER 20

Paige

"Why are you here?" I asked my parents in a tremulous voice as I seated myself in Trace's den.

Sebastian had quickly ushered all of us into Trace's home, and after a quick hello to our host and hostess, he'd hurried the four of us to the den.

I was still so astonished that I'd barely been able to mutter a hello to Trace and Eva.

I still didn't understand why my parents were here in Trace's home. We didn't have any close family, so I was hoping it wasn't some dire news that they felt they had to deliver in person.

"Sebastian invited us," my dad answered quietly. "And your mom and I wanted to see you."

I looked from one to parent to the other, noticing that Dennis and Maria Rutledge looked much the same as they had the last time I saw them. However, I couldn't help but observe the fine lines on their faces, and their anxious expressions. They were seated directly across from me on a plush sofa, so it wasn't difficult to see the subtle changes that had happened over the years.

I turned my head to the right, gaping at Sebastian, who was seated next to me on the loveseat. "Why? You knew we haven't spoken to each other in years?" I felt slightly betrayed, and more than a little bewildered.

He shrugged. "That's why. You miss them, Paige. You know you do. And I think you're a little readier to listen to what they have to say. I knew you'd probably be pissed, and I could even understand why. But I want you to be happy."

"He called us," Maria said, nervously clasping her hands together on her lap. "Paige, I know you're angry, but I'm not sure it's for the right reasons. Sebastian said that you think we were worried about your dad losing his job."

"Weren't you?" I asked hesitantly. "You wanted me to keep my assault a dirty little secret."

"I don't work for Talmage anymore, honey," my dad spoke up. "I haven't since Justin assaulted you. Did you really think I could stay there after what happened?"

"He. Raped. Me." I said each word clearly. I knew my parents didn't like the word, but rape was exactly what happened.

My mom started to cry, tears trickling down her cheeks as she acknowledged, "I know, baby. I know. Do you know how hard it was to know that we couldn't protect you from that, and that we couldn't even help you find justice?"

My dad wrapped his arm around my mother's shoulders as he spoke, "Maybe it wasn't right, but you were our sweet girl, and we wanted to protect you. There was no evidence, and no apparent witnesses. It was your word against Justin's. The Talmage family would have torn you apart, and stripped every bit of your dignity by trying to make you the guilty one. It wasn't that we didn't want Justin to pay, or that we gave a damn about what happened to us. We're your parents, Paige. We just wanted you safe."

I blinked, surprised I'd actually heard any kind of curse word from my dad. "Did you believe me?" I had to ask the question. I needed to know.

"Yes, of course we did," my mother replied, looking like she'd never even doubted my account of the incident for an instant.

My father nodded. "You never lied to us, Paige. Why would we not believe you?"

Oh, God. Maybe they really had been trying to protect me.

Granted, I hadn't understood their stance at the time, but Sebastian was right. I was older, wiser, and much less traumatized now. "I was angry," I explained quietly. "All I wanted was for Justin to pay for all I suffered that night: the fear, the humiliation, the helplessness I felt when I couldn't do anything but be at his mercy. And he had none. He hurt me physically and tormented me emotionally," I said on a loud sob.

"We know, sweetheart, and your mom and I are both so sorry. We were both so upset that anybody had hurt our little girl that we didn't handle it very well. We didn't talk to you about it because we couldn't handle it. That wasn't fair to you." My father's voice was cracking with emotion.

I shook my head. "I shouldn't have run away. If I needed to talk, I should have told you." I was beginning to realize my own mistakes. Maybe my parents hadn't handled my rape very well, but our misunderstanding wasn't all their fault. "I was angry, and not being able to go to the police made me feel helpless and terrified. I felt betrayed because you wanted to hush everything up, and that meant I had to hide all of my pain inside me."

"We blamed ourselves because we had a hard time hearing about what happened," my dad confessed.

I swiped at the still-falling tears on my cheeks as I asked, "You're really not working for Talmage? Where did you go?"

My father shot me a sad smile. "To his biggest competitor. I'm actually a lot happier there."

"So it worked out okay?" I asked anxiously.

"No, sweetheart, it didn't. My baby girl was still hurting, and we didn't know how to talk to you."

I rose, stepping around the coffee table to kneel beside the couch. I clasped both of their hands as I said shakily, "I'm sorry. I thought the worst. I understand now that you were trying to protect me. You were both right. I would have never won the case, and I'm sure I would have been an object of ridicule."

My mom stroked my hair as she looked at me with love in a pair of blue eyes so much like my own. "We're sorry, too, baby. So very sorry. You should have never had to live through what Justin did to you."

My dad squeezed my hand. "We missed you so much," he said with regret in his voice.

"I missed you both, too," I acknowledged with a sob of pain.

My mom stood up and urged me to my feet for a big, Italian hug. "Forgive us. And don't go away again," she whispered urgently in my ear once she'd wrapped me in her embrace.

Dad got up and pulled us both into his body for a group hug as we all cried. But, for me, it was a cleansing, emotionally charged moment that seemed to lift a weight off my shoulders that I hadn't even realized I carried.

"I hope you're going to forgive me, too," a husky voice commented behind me.

I turned, viewing the concern in Sebastian's eyes as he stood off to the side, with his hands in the pockets of his jeans.

I quickly kissed both of my parents' cheeks, then threw myself into Sebastian's arms, momentarily surprising him before he wrapped his strong arms around me.

"Thank you," I whispered fervently into his ear.

"You're welcome. Thank fuck you're not going to hold this against me. I didn't want to force it. But I thought you were ready," he said in a low voice beside my ear.

"I was," I acknowledged. "I guess I just didn't know how to go to them myself and mend our differences."

Sebastian picked me up and twirled me around before setting me back on my feet again. "Happy Thanksgiving, babe."

"Happy Thanksgiving, Sebastian," I said in a quiet but firm voice, hugging his strong body tightly.

We broke apart reluctantly, and I officially introduced him to my parents. The conversation flowed so easily that it was like we'd never been at odds with each other.

Mom caught me up on all of the gossip from home, and my dad told me about his new job, and told me about a college fund he'd saved to help me pay my student loans in the future.

I shook my head. "No, Dad. Use it for your retirement. I got this amazing job working for a very big, important company," I told him in a teasing voice. "They pay fairly decent. I think I can handle it."

Sebastian spoke out in a similarly joking tone. "Fairly decent?"

"Well, I am a Harvard grad," I reminded him.

"I noticed. Do we need to give you a raise, Ms. Rutledge?" His eyes were teaming with mischief.

I pretended to think about his question. "Maybe not yet. I'm still fairly new. I have to prove myself."

"Not to me," Sebastian answered in a raspy voice. "I know every one of your assets."

I coughed hard to keep from laughing, knowing my parents didn't quite understand what was going on. I looked him up and down, caressing him with my eyes. "And I know every one of yours, Mr. Walker."

His eyes turned dangerously fiery as he wrapped his arms around my waist from behind. "Your daughter is amazing," he said to my parents.

My mother beamed, and Dad nodded. "We know that," Mom said with a smile. "I hope we'll be invited to the wedding."

"Mom...we aren't...we don't...we—"

"When the time comes, we hope you'll be participating," Sebastian interrupted smoothly. "I need to get a ring on her finger first."

"If she's playing hard-to-get, I might be able to give you some pointers," my dad offered. "Her mother was stubborn, too."

My mother batted her husband playfully on the arm. "I was no such thing. And Paige has done just fine without you grilling her boyfriend."

"We'll talk later, Dennis," Sebastian said in a conspiratorial tone.

I rolled my eyes, but leaned back against Sebastian's large body, grateful for his support.

Yeah, maybe I should be angry, but I knew if I had been left to deal with my parents on my own, it may have taken a very long time to get the courage to approach them.

A sharp knock on the door made all of us startle, then we all laughed.

"Hey. It's Thanksgiving, and the master chef is ready for her guests." Trace stood at the door with a smile on his face.

"On our way," Sebastian assured Trace.

The four of us were still chattering, making small talk and cracking jokes as we followed Trace to the table.

My heart was full as I let Sebastian lead me to my chair. "Where is Dane?" I asked curiously.

"He couldn't make it," Trace answered from across the table. "He got sick, and now he's trying to finish an important commissioned piece on time. Dane's been taking on more and more projects. I think he needs some help."

"I'm so sorry," I said, speaking to no one in particular. I was fairly certain that Sebastian, Trace, and Eva felt Dane's absence.

"It was his choice," Eva rebutted as she entered the dining room. "I told him he was missing out."

I instantly thought of Kenzie. "Well, if he ever needs an assistant, I know somebody who would kill to work for him. She loves his art, and she's an artist herself. She has a lot of natural talent, but she's never been able to do much formal study. Honestly, I haven't met Dane, but I think they'd have a lot in common."

I saw Sebastian and Trace trade a rather scheming look before we all sat down to eat, and I wondered what it was all about, but it was soon forgotten as everyone joined in the conversation. I consumed enormous quantities of food as I watched my parents finally relax, obviously realizing that although the Walkers were rich, they were also genuine.

Eva's meal was by far the best I'd ever had, every dish prepared with an obvious love for good food.

Looking around the table as we all groaned at the thought of pie, but accepted it anyway, I realized how much my life was changing, and just how much I had to be thankful for.

CHAPTER 21

Paige

Two weeks later, my life was so good that it was almost frightening. Every day I gained a little more of myself back again. I was losing the need to constantly be in control, and I'd actually done a few things spontaneously. Granted, it was nothing big and exciting, but day by day, the real Paige was coming back, and what's more...I liked her.

I was growing so close to Sebastian that it was almost painful. Every day he did something to make me smile, and every night he rocked my world.

I was ready to pinch myself to make sure I was actually sitting in a hot spring in the middle of winter, outdoors, and completely naked with the hottest man I'd ever met. Rocky Springs, the secluded resort that belonged to Sebastian's cousins and his aunt Aileen, was the most beautiful area of Colorado I'd ever seen. Of course, I hadn't seen much in other areas, but I was willing to bet nothing much could top our current location.

Sebastian had snagged us a "cabin" for the weekend, which was actually more like a fancy hotel suite disguised by cedar logs. We'd arrived earlier in the day and I'd squealed like a child when

I'd ridden on the back of a snowmobile with him. I'd quickly learned that his need for power and speed in a transport wasn't limited to automobiles.

"Having fun?" Sebastian asked, his hand stroking lazily on my belly as I lounged back against him.

The water felt heavenly. The air was frigid, but we were warm and cozy in the hot spring. I dreaded getting out and making a run for the door, but I wasn't going to think about that when I was laying with Sebastian, gazing at the stars.

"This is incredible," I answered honestly. "It seems so strange to be so warm outside in the middle of winter."

"Now you can tell Kenzie that you actually have been in the hot springs at the best resort in Colorado."

"She'll love that," I mused.

"You miss her?" It was more of a statement than a question.

"I do."

"What about your parents?"

I wasn't quite used to the fact that I was rebuilding my relationship with my mom and dad, but we talked every day since they'd returned to the East Coast, and I knew we were going to be okay. "I miss them, too."

"Lonely?" he questioned.

I turned around to face him in the dim light, making sure I kept my body in the water. "No. I don't think I'll ever be lonely when I'm with you."

He grinned, as though I'd made him the happiest guy in the world. God...how I loved this man. Sebastian had turned my world upside down, but in a good way. Maybe I wasn't always in control anymore, but being with him was worth it, and I trusted him completely.

My heart ached as I wrapped my arms around his neck and felt our bodies connect as I straddled him. "I love you," I said breathlessly.

"Fuck! It's about time you said that, woman," he rasped, his hand wrapping firmly around the back of my neck to pull my mouth to his.

Need sizzled through my body as Sebastian devoured my mouth in a raw expression of desperation. I relaxed and melted into him, threading my hands into his hair and fisting the coarse locks.

I suddenly realized that I'd never told him I loved him. He'd said those words to me at Thanksgiving, but I'd never spoken them aloud to Sebastian.

When he'd finally kissed me senseless, he moved his dangerous mouth to my neck, nipping and teasing the sensitive skin.

"I love you. I love you. I love you," I was chanting the words, the relief I felt in saying them completely intoxicating.

His arms tightened around me. "I love you, too, babe. So fucking much it hurts."

"Love should never hurt," I whispered into his ear.

"Don't worry. It hurts so damn good," he answered in a deep, sensual voice that made my heart clench.

His wicked mouth descended to my pebbled nipples, my breasts now just above the surface of the water. I moaned and leaned back in his arms, giving him all of the access he wanted.

He teased and bit gently with his teeth, then soothed with his tongue. I suddenly realized what he meant when he said it hurt so damn good. The small pain followed by intense pleasure was enough to make me half crazy.

"Sebastian," I whispered, my voice filled with longing as I held his head against my breasts.

He gave me more, everything and anything I wanted as he continued to alternate from one nipple to the other, making my head spin with desire.

"Fuck me," I demanded, needing him inside me so badly that I couldn't breathe.

He lifted me and pulled me forward. "No, baby. *You* fuck *me*."

"Is this even possible?" I asked hesitantly.

His grin was wicked and seductive. "Oh, yeah."

I had to admit that I loved the weightlessness of the water, but I had to wiggle forward and grasp his cock roughly.

"Christ! Now, Paige," he commanded, his voice raw with need.

I fit our bodies together, then sunk down as hard as I could. Sebastian took control, grasping my hips so he could surge up, sliding inside me and filling me until I moaned with satisfaction. "Yesssss!" I hissed, knowing I'd be content to stay just like this for a very long time.

"Ride me," Sebastian urged, keeping a hard grasp on my hips.

I rose, then sunk back down as he surged up, the resulting sensation incredibly erotic as the warm water caressed my nipples every time I sunk down.

My hands tightened in his hair, and I leaned down to kiss him, desperate for a complete connection.

I didn't want to admit it, but I needed this man completely. Sebastian filled every one of those empty places in my soul that had been exposed after we met.

He'd ripped them open, then repaired every one of them.

The slow ride necessitated by the water was frustrating, yet it drew out our pleasure, making my need build to the point of pain.

I pulled my mouth from his with an urgent scream. "Sebastian!"

"Easy, sweetheart," he rasped. "Let it come."

I rotated my hips, grinding down on his cock, needing the pressure on my clit.

"That's it, Paige. Take it. Take what you want."

"I want you," I whimpered as I kept grinding against him.

"You have me," he vowed huskily. "You have since you dissed me in that elevator."

I rose and sunk down again, my grinding motion more desperate, more urgent.

Sebastian's hands gripped my ass, and he massaged as I rotated my hips in a hypnotic motion, staying on the same rhythm of rising and falling, then rubbing myself against him. The pleasure built with every single move.

I suddenly flinched as I felt Sebastian fingering my anus, slowly sliding a finger into the puckered opening.

"Easy, babe," he crooned. "You know I won't hurt you."

I relaxed, shaking off my old ghosts that told me that there was nothing but pain back there. As he synced his shallow penetration with the rise and fall of my body, I let myself enjoy the carnal sensation of the movement of Sebastian's finger inside me. It didn't hurt. It didn't make me scream with pain. It made me crazy as I became more and more frenzied, the heat in my belly starting to shoot straight to my core.

My climax was different, visceral and all-consuming as it rocked my body and my soul.

"Yes, Sebastian. Yes." I leaned down and joined our mouths, feeling like Sebastian was completely consuming me as he groaned against my lips.

I sunk down so he could fill me one more time, gyrating hard as I crashed down on top of him, his cock as far as it could possibly be inside me.

Sebastian's harsh breathing was all I heard right before my orgasm overwhelmed me, making my entire body quiver as my core clenched down hard on his cock.

As I rode my incredible climax, Sebastian surged inside me a few more times, groaning in agony and ecstasy as he held me against him and let go of his hot release with a tortured curse. "Fuck. Yeah."

We clung to each other, both of us struggling for breath as he pulled me flush against his naked body.

"I love you," I said with a blissful sigh after I'd caught my breath.

Our bodies were meshed together, my arms around his neck and my head resting weary but content on his shoulder.

"I love you, too, Paige," he rasped into my ear in a husky tone.

For once in my life, I knew what it meant to be ecstatically happy. I finally understood the euphoria my classmates and friends used to talk about when they were having conversations about the guys they loved.

"Thank you," I mumbled against his warm skin.

He leaned back to look at my face. "For what?"

"For being you," I whispered. "Thank you for seeing *me*."

How Sebastian had seen things in me that others hadn't was still a mystery to me, but I was grateful he was able to reach into my being and yank the real Paige from my cold and empty soul.

Now, all I could feel was a barrage of emotions, like every feeling I'd ever held back was finally free.

"I saw *you* because I knew *me*," he answered, pulling me back against him and stroking my upper back in a soothing motion. "I ran away from everything for so long that it wasn't hard to see what you were doing. I could feel your warmth, sweetheart, even though you didn't show it. I can't say I'm exactly warm and fuzzy, but I could recognize myself in you."

In his own way, Sebastian was rather hot and very fuzzy. He had a heart of gold buried beneath some lingering cynicism. And he was relentless when he cared about someone.

"I never stood a chance," I grumbled good-naturedly.

"Nope," he agreed amiably. "Not from the moment you walked into that elevator. I was rock-hard almost instantly, and believe it or not, my interest in women was non-existent. I was too caught up in my new projects to care whether or not I got laid. I thought my dick was ready to shrivel up and die off."

I let out a startled, delighted laugh. "I can guarantee it hadn't started to get smaller."

"You saved me," he said with false, amused drama.

I shivered as I smiled, starting to feel the chill in the air now that I was above the water level. A cold wind had started up, and it penetrated the heat that was being thrown off by the mineral pool.

Sebastian, being the observant guy he was, stood up and lifted me into his arms, then sprinted into our cabin through the nearby sliding door.

I squealed as the cold breeze hit my naked body, taking my breath away. "Put me down. I'm no lightweight," I chastised loudly.

"You're a tiny little thing," he argued as he put me back on my feet in the bathroom attached to the master bedroom. "We have to rinse off."

I watched as he adjusted the water in the massive shower enclosure, admiring the strength and beauty of his naked body. He was perfectly formed and muscular, and I admired his rock-hard ass as he turned his back to get the water to a perfect temperature.

Unable to stop myself, I moved forward and pressed myself against his back, wrapping my arms around him and resting my head against his warm skin. "Sometimes I wonder how this happened?" I questioned aloud.

He turned slowly, then lifted his hand to release my messy hair from its confining clip, watching intently as the cascading locks fell around my shoulders. "Fate," he said, his expression intense, his eyes dark with some emotion I couldn't exactly name.

"Do you believe in destiny?" I asked curiously.

He kissed my forehead and clasped my hand. "I never did before, but I'm starting to think it exists. I'm a science guy. I only believed in things I could prove, analyze, or touch."

"What happened?" I asked uncertainly.

"I met you," he answered simply.

I smiled at him. "That's it?"

"You were all I needed to prove to me that there are some things that can't always be explained rationally. All I knew is that I needed you."

My chest ached at his words. Sebastian wasn't a flowery type of man, so those earnest words meant everything to me. "I needed you, too," I replied in a breathless voice.

Our connection was elemental, simple yet intensely complicated if we wanted to keep driving ourselves crazy about why we fit.

I didn't want to wonder about that anymore. I just wanted to make Sebastian as happy as he made me.

He tugged on my hand, leading me into the spray of clean water. "Bring on the magic," he said, sounding amused.

I wanted to tell him that for me, the magic was already here. It was him. It was the way he cared about me, worried about me, did everything possible to fix my broken spirit.

Words escaped me as I followed him into the shower, but it didn't matter. The moment I leaned into him and kissed him, the magic was right there for both of us.

CHAPTER 22

Paige

I suppose it was inevitable that I'd eventually have to fall off cloud nine and back into the real world.

It happened a few days later when Sebastian and I were back in Denver, lazily lying on his living room couch, listening to the nightly news.

My body tensed as I heard Justin Talmage mentioned by a newscaster in breaking news. My sleepy state vanished, and I bolted upright as his picture flashed across the screen. I watched in horror as the story was reported, knowing immediately exactly what had happened.

Sebastian sat up and wrapped his arms around me, staying silent until the story was over.

I was trembling as he shut off the television, stunned and horrified by what I'd just heard.

"He did it to her. I know he did. They can say her condition is under investigation, but it's bullshit. He overdosed that woman and probably raped her," I said angrily.

"No wonder I haven't been able to find the bastard," Sebastian said furiously. "He was hiding out in another college town here in Colorado looking for prey."

"Were you looking for him?"

"Hell, yes. I've been trying to nail down his location since I found out what happened."

I shivered, glad that Sebastian had never found Justin. "Why?"

"He needs to be stopped," he answered in a dangerous tone.

"I know. But not your way," I told him firmly.

I knew instantly what I needed to do. The news report had featured a college female that Justin had supposedly found in her apartment close to death. There was little information yet, but I had no doubt that Justin hadn't "found" the woman in that condition. He'd *caused* it. The moment I'd heard that they were investigating drugs as a possible reason for her near-death state in a Colorado college town, I had no doubt that Justin didn't find her that way. He'd overdosed her himself.

"Bastard!" I cursed as I rose to my feet. "I wasn't a single case, Sebastian. He's still drugging and raping women. He's just gotten away with it." I went to find my jacket. "I need to go. I need to see her."

Sebastian grasped my arm to stop me. "She's in critical condition, Paige."

"Then I'll talk to her parents. Please. I have to do this."

He eyed my expression stoically. "I can't watch you go through this all over again," he answered in a raw, hoarse voice that was filled with concern.

My eyes pleaded with him as I shook off his grip. "Then don't. I can go alone. She's not that far away."

"Fuck! That's not what I meant. My ass will be right beside you wherever you go. But it will kill me if you have to go through more pain because of Talmage."

I shook my head, my eyes staying focused on his. "It's time, Sebastian. It doesn't have to be painful. This isn't about me anymore. It's about her. I know what it's like to be where she is right now. If they have no clue that Justin is actually responsible, any evidence might disappear."

I could see the muscle in his jaw twitching, like he was clenching his teeth as he slowly nodded. "Let's go. But if I see Talmage, I can't guarantee I won't kill the bastard myself."

"I might need your help," I told him as he helped me into my coat and grabbed his own from the back of a chair.

"We'll get to whoever we need to in order to find out what happened," he vowed. "I'll call Blake if I need to. He's a senator with a lot of powerful connections."

I nodded jerkily, knowing that having extended family as well-connected as Blake could come in handy to make people listen.

I'd use any advantage I could get.

We were out of the house and on the road within minutes, speeding toward the hospital where Justin's latest victim was fighting for her life.

I didn't have time for remorse, or wishing that I could have stopped Justin years ago. I was dealing with exactly what was occurring right now, and it would have to be enough.

It took two days before I could see Julie and speak to her. As I sat at her bedside, I felt my heart squeeze tightly in my chest, the young woman reminding me so much of myself five years ago.

Sebastian had been my rock during the last forty-eight hours, staying with me in a nearby hotel as we contacted every person we could to make sure evidence was gathered at the hospital to find out whether or not the young woman had been sexually abused. Toxicology had automatically been ordered since they weren't sure if she was under the influence of drugs.

"I didn't even know him," Julie said timidly after everyone else had left the room so I could talk to her alone.

The girl was pretty and unassuming. I didn't know how she'd been at the bar where she'd encountered Justin, but she looked small and terrified in a hospital gown, and almost as white as the hospital sheets.

I reached out and clasped her hand. "It will be okay. You have all the support you need," I said firmly. "Tell me what happened."

I knew she'd already given as much information to the police as she could, and they had recovered DNA when they'd done a rape exam before she'd awakened from her overdose. The toxicology report had shown evidence of one of the common date-rape drugs.

"I wish I remembered more, but I passed out almost immediately," she explained hesitantly. "Justin offered to buy me a drink, and I took it. I drank it pretty fast because I was thirsty from dancing. All I can remember is him helping me get outside, and I remember him undressing me in a fancy limo. After that, things are pretty hazy."

"You might eventually remember more," I said in a gentle voice. "It took me a while to recall some of the things that happened to me, and I still don't remember everything."

"I'm not sure I want to remember," she said tearfully. "Maybe it's better if I don't. Why would he do something like this? I never encouraged him. In fact, I said no when he asked me to leave with him."

"That's why he drugged you," I explained. "He claims you were an acquaintance, and he found you passed out."

"I never saw him before that night, and he introduced himself only by his first name in the bar. He wanted me to go with him, but I didn't want to. I wasn't sure why he was even hanging around. I was there with my friends, and I have a boyfriend. I'd never cheat on him."

I knew Sebastian was already talking to Julie's boyfriend, trying to help him cope with and support the woman he loved.

I adored him for what he was doing, and his insight into what Julie's best support system would need to help her.

"I know," I told her softly.

"Did he really do this to you, too?" Julie questioned.

I nodded. "I washed away evidence because I never went into the hospital. By the time I finally got it together, I had nothing except my word against Justin's, and his father is a powerful man."

"I never thought something like this would happen to me," she said tearfully.

"Neither of us did. It's always something we think will happen to some poor girl on the news. But it did happen, and Justin has to be shut down for good. We can't let this happen to one more woman," I said in a strong, determined tone.

"We won't," Julie answered, squeezing my hand. "If you're strong enough to tell your story, I can, too."

"There are others," I told her, hoping it would help to know she wasn't alone. Two more women had spoken out about Justin since the news had broken that Justin Talmage was most likely the culprit for Julie's condition.

Like me, they seemed to find the strength to fight now that they knew they weren't alone, and realized that Justin had to be stopped.

"Are you afraid to talk about it?" Julie whispered.

I slowly shook my head. "No. Not anymore. I have a wonderful man in my life now, and he understands and supports me. Believe me, it helps."

"Julie has one, too," a young male voice said from the entrance of the hospital room.

I watched as the young woman smiled and exclaimed loudly, "Brad!"

Julie's boyfriend had obviously finished his conversation with Sebastian. I stood, squeezing the woman's hand one last time before I moved to the doorway. "I'll leave you two alone."

Brad nodded as he said quietly, "Thank you for everything."

"No need to thank me," I responded in a quiet voice. "I'm finally doing the right thing."

I stepped past him and moved down the hallway, exiting through the main entrance of the hospital.

The minute I took my first breath of fresh air, I was mobbed by reporters. I was due to give a public statement, and there wasn't a single bit of hesitancy as I waited for the cameras to start rolling and all of the microphones to be shoved near my face.

I smiled weakly as I saw Sebastian and my parents push through the crowd to be by my side. They were flanking me in moments, and I took a deep breath as a female reporter asked me to tell them who I was and what had happened to me.

I felt Sebastian's arm curl around my waist, and my mom take my hand on the other side. My dad supported my mother, just like Sebastian was comforting me.

I took a deep breath and answered the query. "My name is Paige Rutledge, and five years ago, Justin Talmage drugged me, assaulted me, and raped me."

The questions came one after the other, and I answered them as honestly as I could. After a few minutes, Sebastian grumbled that I was done answering their questions, and he shouldered his way through the crowd, making a path for me and my parents to follow.

"You okay?" Sebastian leaned down to ask, his voice filled with both anger and concern.

Strangely, I felt better than I'd felt in a long time. I was stronger, freer, and more determined than I'd ever been. My heart bled for the women who had suffered at Justin's hands, but I was confident in the hope that he'd never hurt another female again.

"I'm good," I answered as all four of us climbed into his vehicle and made a rapid getaway.

When he got on the freeway, his hand reached for mine, and I sighed as our fingers entwined.

"Then let's get the hell out of here and go home," he rumbled.

I leaned back against the seat and relaxed, knowing I'd never heard any sweeter words than that.

CHAPTER 23

Paige

"Are you really leaving Walker?" Eva asked curiously as we sat in one of our favorite restaurants several weeks later.

Trace Walker's wife had become one of my biggest supporters, and a friend. We'd made it a point to meet for lunch every Saturday, and I spoke to her on the phone nearly every day. Today, the Walker brothers had needed to go look at a property they'd found that might meet Sebastian's needs for a headquarters in his solar venture. So Eva and I were alone.

I took a sip of my water to wash down the amazing burrito I was consuming before I answered, "Your brother-in-law fired me."

"Sebastian?" Eva exclaimed, her eyes widening as she looked at me in surprise.

"Yep."

"Why in the world would he do that?"

I shrugged. "Because he knew I wasn't doing the job I wanted to do."

Eva shook her head. "I don't understand. I thought you loved Walker."

"I love a Walker, but not the corporation," I said teasingly. "Sebastian knew I always wanted to defend people who couldn't afford to defend themselves. He talked to Blake, and the senator helped me find a job in government public service here in Denver."

Eva frowned. "But doesn't it pay a lot less?"

"It does," I agreed. "But they have a loan forgiveness program that can help me get my student loan debt manageable. I have to pay on an income-based level, and eventually, all of the loans are forgiven when I've worked in public service for the required amount of time. It kind of washes out. My payments are so high right now that I end up giving a big chunk of my paycheck to student loan debt. And I really, really want this new job. It might be thankless at times, but it's more rewarding. I always wanted to be a lawyer to help people get justice. That means more to me now than it ever has."

"I understand," Eva murmured in agreement. "I'm surprised that Sebastian hasn't already paid off your loans. He's crazy about you."

"He tried," I said with a smile. "I had to put my foot down. We were supposed to just be trying out our relationship. I don't want him paying my bills. I knew I'd have loans to pay back. It's my responsibility."

Eva rolled her eyes. "You two have been trying each other out for a while now. I think Sebastian was sold a long time ago. There's no way he's going to let you go."

"I don't want him to," I answered bluntly.

"I noticed," she said with a grin before she started eating again.

We ate in silence for a few minutes before I spoke again. "I'm happy about the new job. And Sebastian didn't technically fire me according to my employment records. It took me a while to realize that money isn't necessarily power, and it doesn't take the place of doing what you love to do."

"Then I'm definitely happy for you." Eva hesitated before adding, "I'm married to one of the wealthiest men in the world, but Trace knows I want to work. He never wants to keep me from doing what I love. I wouldn't know what to do with myself if I didn't work."

"Me either," I admitted, even though I wasn't in Eva's position. There was no way I could even contemplate not having my own career.

We chatted as we leisurely finished our lunch, our topic of conversation finally coming to the third Walker brother.

Eva sighed. "I'm worried about Dane. He never showed up for any of the holidays, and he sounds so lonely over the phone. He needs somebody there with him on that island."

"What if he wants to be alone?" I mused. "What if he doesn't want company?"

"He does. And he's gotten so busy that he needs an assistant to help out, but he won't admit it. I have no idea if he's taking care of himself, or if he even stops to eat. Trace says he doesn't cook."

I smiled, knowing that for a chef like Eva, not eating much was definitely serious business. But honestly, I worried about the solitary Walker brother, too, even though I didn't know him personally.

Our talk moved to other subjects, and we stayed way too long after we finished eating. Checking my beautiful watch from Sebastian, I noticed that the time had flown by, and that Trace and his brother were probably home by now.

Eva dropped me off at Sebastian's home with a wave and a promise to get together again next week before she drove away.

I searched through my purse for my keys as I stood at the front door. Sebastian had given me my own key, and I practically lived at his house. My apartment was pretty much silent and unoccupied.

Just as I wrapped my hand around the keychain at the bottom of my bag, the door flew open and Sebastian snatched me from the doorstep, sweeping me up into his muscular arms.

"Hello, beautiful. I missed you," he said huskily in my ear as he held me close and spun me around.

I giggled, something that I tried very hard not to do often, and weakly protested for him to put me down.

He set me on my feet inside the door and closed it behind me.

I stripped off my jacket as I looked at him anxiously. "Well… tell me? Was it good?"

"It was better than good. It was fucking fantastic. We already made the deal, and we should be able to get rolling very soon."

I let out a loud whoop and threw myself back into his arms. "I'm so happy for you," I said enthusiastically.

Sebastian wanted me to be happy, but I was desperately hoping he would find a place so he could do what he wanted, too.

He held me tightly, then kissed me, a long, tender embrace that warmed more than just my body. It touched my heart.

"I love you," he said huskily. "Marry me, Paige."

His comment was so unexpected that I was taken aback. "What?"

He leaned back so he could look at my face. His hand stroked through my unbound hair, then tilted my chin up until our eyes locked. "I said marry me."

"Was that a request or an order?" I teased.

"It was a request if you're saying 'yes.' If you want to think about it, then it's an order," he answered, the nervous tone of his voice belying his words.

"I thought we wanted to keep this uncomplicated."

"Naw. Let's complicate the hell out of it," he suggested hopefully as he dug into the pocket of his jeans and pulled out a beautiful red velvet box, then popped open the lid. "Marry me?"

I stared at the enormous diamond set in platinum, my eyes growing wide as the gem sparkled under the lights. "Oh, God. It's beautiful," I said with awe, my eyes filling with tears.

"Say you'll marry me already," Sebastian complained. "You're killing me here."

"Yes!" I cried out, the tears spilling rapidly from my eyes. "Yes."

"Thank fuck," Sebastian said, his relief evident in his voice as he took the ring from the box and slid it onto my finger.

"It's the perfect size."

"I asked your mother," he said mischievously. "I was going to take you out for a romantic dinner and then ask, but I couldn't wait any longer. You've been mine since the moment you stepped into that elevator at Walker. I need it to be official."

I wrapped my arms around his neck, savoring the weight of his ring on my finger as a symbol of his love. "Have we ever done anything normal?"

"Not yet," he answered with a grin.

I kissed him tenderly, knowing I'd savor this moment for the rest of my life. I never expected him to want to marry me right now, but I certainly never considered saying no. Sebastian meant everything to me, and I couldn't imagine life without him anymore.

The tenderness sparked quickly to passion as he took control of the embrace, holding the back of my head while he devoured my mouth.

"I need you, Paige," he said gutturally when he'd pulled his mouth from mine.

"I'm already yours," I told him honestly.

He grasped my ass, and I hopped up and wrapped my legs around his waist, desperate to have him inside me. "Fuck me, Sebastian. No foreplay, no teasing, no waiting."

Putting my feet back on the ground, I started to strip off my clothes, watching as Sebastian desperately did the same. He finished first, then moved close to me and pulled strategically at my panties, stripping them from my body easily and painlessly.

"Again?" I groaned, knowing he'd just destroyed another pair of the expensive lingerie he'd given me.

"I'll get you more," he rumbled as his hands roamed my body possessively.

I couldn't get out anything except a moan as his fingers roamed between my thighs, then expertly slid through my folds and straight to my slick clit. "Jesus, Paige. You're always ready and wet for me."

I couldn't argue with him. My body responded to him just as readily as his did to me. "Fuck me, Sebastian. Make all of this real."

My head was still spinning from his proposal, and all I wanted to do was get him inside me. My heart, body, and soul needed him to confirm what I already knew to be true.

We belonged together. I didn't know if it was fate. But like Sebastian, I was beginning to think we had always been meant for each other.

"This is all very real, babe," he drawled as my back hit the wall.

"Now," I demanded, tightening my grip around his waist in a silent plea for him to join our bodies together.

He didn't hesitate to surge forward and impale himself inside me with enough force to make me cry out. "Sebastian. Oh, God. Yes. Please."

My body was clamoring for him, and I inhaled his intoxicating scent as he buried his cock to the root inside me.

It was a frenzied, uncontrolled madness that took both of us over as Sebastian pummeled his cock in and out of my slick channel, fucking me like he had to do it or die.

My climax built so quickly that it left me breathless, panting for release. We surged together, Sebastian positioning me so every stroke rubbed against my engorged clit, building a pressure that was almost painful. "I can't wait," I whimpered, grinding against him as he slammed into me.

"Then don't," he groaned. "This. Is. Real."

I plunged my fingers into his hair and gripped it hard as my orgasm took control, tossing me around in the waves of pleasure that came flooding through my body and permeated my heart.

Holding on tight, my release so intense, I bit down on his shoulder as our bodies continued to rock together.

"Oh, fuck. I love it when you do that," he groaned, hammering harder as we both hurdled toward release.

The sounds of our harsh breathing filled the air as we clung to each other, absorbing the final ripples of pleasure from our volatile orgasms. Sebastian stumbled to the couch with our bodies still connected, only allowing us to be separated when he flopped onto his back on the sofa and pulled me on top of him.

We were both slick with sweat as I tried to slow down my breathing and calm my racing heart.

"That *was* real," I teased when I'd finally caught my breath.

"Very," he agreed as he slapped me playfully on the ass.

"I love you so much," I whispered breathlessly, resting my hands beside his head to push myself up.

His eyes caressed my face, his intense expression telling me everything I needed to know.

Staring down at the man who had literally changed my life, I realized that our meeting couldn't be an accident. How did one find exactly what they needed at just the right time?

I craved this beautiful man like I needed oxygen to breathe.

"I love you, sweetheart," he finally responded, his tone heavy with emotion.

We skipped the fancy dinner and ate hotdogs at home. Then we spent the night sealing the deal on our engagement completely naked, which in my opinion was much more pleasurable than getting dressed for dinner.

CHAPTER 24

Sebastian

"How's the plans going for the new property?" Trace asked as I sat in his office a week after I'd gotten engaged to Paige.

"Good. Really good." The purchase was progressing, and the details on design and usage of the space was being finalized. "I think it's a better site than the New Mexico lot, and it's closer to Denver, so I can be out on site more often."

"How's Paige?" Trace asked.

"Mine." Putting that ring on her finger was the best damn thing I'd ever done. But it still didn't stop the urgent desire I had to insulate her from anything that would hurt her in the future. "I'm completely obsessed about her happiness, which I find pretty uncomfortable," I admitted to Trace unhappily.

He looked at me curiously. "Why?"

I shrugged. "It's not fucking normal. I almost hate the fact that I pushed her into taking a new job. I can't see her. I can't make sure she's okay. It might make me crazy."

Trace let out a booming laugh. "That's how it is when you're madly in love," he said, amused.

"I do love her. So much that I'm not sure it's healthy."

"There's nothing wrong with wanting her to be happy, Sebastian. And there's no crime in missing her. Hell, I still get irritated when I don't see Eva in the morning."

"I know." Trace could be a real asshole if he didn't at least get to kiss his wife goodbye in the morning. "Oh, hell. I'm starting to act exactly like you," I grumbled, suddenly noticing the similarities.

"Welcome to my world," Trace said drily. "You'll live through it. It just feels like you won't sometimes. Paige is worth it."

I was quiet as I considered his words. Really, Paige was worth *any* sacrifice. And she was happy. I just wished I didn't miss her so damn much. "Maybe I'll feel more secure when we're married."

Trace shook his head. "Nope. You'll worry even more because you'll have a new level of connection."

Now that I thought about it, Trace had become worse about his obsession with his wife after the wedding. "I'm fucked," I replied in a graveled voice.

"Then don't marry her," Trace replied lightly as he took a swallow of coffee from his mug.

"Not happening. I was sweating bullets about whether or not she'd say 'yes.' I'm not going through that shit again."

Sometimes I still wondered how a player like me could end up with a fiancée like Paige. She was the type of woman who cried over getting something as simple as a new watch or lingerie… or even a new coat. Yeah, she'd always say it was just because I was thinking about her, but I'd never known a woman who gave a damn if I was thinking of her. With other women, it was the gift, and the price that counted. But not my fiancée. With her, it really was the thought that counted.

I was rock-hard in seconds as my mind drifted off to the night we got engaged…

"Sebastian!" Trace shouted.

I looked at him guiltily. "Yeah."

"You were somewhere else," Trace concluded.

"Yeah. For a minute. What did you say?"

My brother gave me a knowing look before he said, "Is Dane going to make it for the wedding?"

"He'd better," I grumbled. "Or I'll go drag him off his island."

I wanted my younger brother present to share my happiness. I sure as hell was only getting married once, and I wanted all the witnesses I could get.

"I don't think you'll need to. I executed our plan," Trace said quietly. "I think you're right. He needs help in more ways than one. I know he's busy, but I think he's using his success as an excuse to avoid the world entirely. Even his family."

I nodded. I wasn't sure how Paige was going to like our plan, but I didn't think she'd object to us helping her best friend and my brother.

"He'll kill us if it doesn't work," I pointed out to Trace.

"Well, at least he'd have to leave his island for that," my older brother said with a grin.

I smirked back at him. "Yeah. He will. I hope Kenzie can bring him back to life again."

"She sounded excited about a new job, especially one that pays a lot of money, and involves Dane's art career. The only thing she didn't sound happy about was leaving the city."

I frowned. "Yeah. Paige mentioned that she liked the city life."

"But she seemed more than willing to deal with that."

I had yet to meet Paige's best friend, but I knew she could use the money, and she had the skills and experience to help Dane. In fact, I was fairly sure she could understand my younger brother better than we did right now.

"Good. I—"

"What in the world did you two do to my best friend?" An angry female voice that I recognized instantly sounded from the entrance of Trace's office.

"Paige?" I said, confused as I turned to see her standing just inside the door. She looked beautiful in a light blue dress and heels, her hair up in a considerably less stark hairdo.

Christ! She looked fucking amazing. Unfortunately, she also looked pissed.

She ignored me as she approached Trace's desk. "You sent my best friend to some remote island somewhere?"

Trace calmly motioned to the chair next to mine. "Please sit. She wasn't supposed to tell you until Sebastian had a chance to let you know first."

She sat on the edge of the chair, then demanded, "Talk! Tell me why you sent my friend off to the middle of nowhere. And it better be good. Kenzie hasn't had the easiest life. And I had to take some time away from a new job I love to find out what you're doing."

One thing I loved about my fiancée was the fact that she fiercely defended someone she cared about, or people that she felt were being taken advantage of. I still adored that trait, but right now, I was wishing she'd be a little less defensive. But that wasn't going to happen. Paige was born to fight for those who couldn't.

"I was going to tell you," I confessed. "We were trying to help Kenzie, not hurt her. Trace and I offered her a job as Dane's assistant. She's getting paid a small fortune, which I think she could use. She doesn't have to pay the expenses of living in the city, and it will help my little brother. You said she loved his work, and would love to work with him. So we made her a proposition."

"One she couldn't refuse, I suppose," Paige said with a sigh. "She loves living in the city. She'll hate living on an island with nobody to talk to. Will I even be able to talk to her?"

"She'll have Dane. And yes, you can still talk to her. Maybe he'd be willing to work with her on her art," Trace suggested.

I watched Paige cross her arms and she shot me and Trace a warning gaze. "How does Dane feel about her coming to work with him?"

The office went quiet, the crickets chirping as I searched desperately for an answer that wasn't a lie.

"Oh, God. He doesn't know?"

More crickets that went on and on.

"It's better this way," Trace said firmly. "Dane is retreating from the world. But once Kenzie shows up, I'm hoping he'll pull out of that."

"She could end up hurt," Paige answered angrily. "Did that ever occur to either one of you?"

"If Dane rejects her, then we'll still pay her," I said insistently, not wanting Paige to think we'd throw her best friend to the wolves.

"It's not about the money." Paige looked at me accusingly. "I've told you some of Kenzie's history. If he rejects her, she'll feel even worse than she already does about herself. It took her a long time to accept what happened to her. It turned her whole world upside down, and not in a good way."

Honestly, I hadn't thought about Kenzie's feelings. "We thought we were helping them both," I answered huskily.

"Dane won't hurt her," Trace said quietly.

"Maybe not physically—"

"Not emotionally, either." Trace's expression was thoughtful as he continued. "Our little brother has been through too many of his own challenges, and even though he won't admit it, he's lonely and hurt. He won't do that to somebody else."

Paige sighed. "I hope you're right. It's not that I don't want her to have every opportunity she can get, but I'm worried about her living in a hut somewhere in the wilderness. She's my best friend, and the only person who had my back for years."

I wanted to remind Paige that there were any number of people who were there for her now, including me. But it didn't make up for the years she'd had to struggle alone. "A hut?" I finally questioned.

"I'm assuming this place is remote." Paige glanced at me, then at Trace.

"It's remote, but it's far from primitive," Trace explained. "Dane has all the niceties any person could want, and some that Kenzie has never even thought about."

I watched an expression of relief spread across Paige's beautiful face. "She sounded excited, especially about meeting and working with Dane. But I don't want her to be disappointed."

"She won't," I assured Paige confidently. "She can come with Dane to our wedding. If she's the least bit miserable, we will find her something else, something a hell of a lot better than being employed with odd jobs in New York."

"You're right. She wasn't in a good position," Paige admitted. "But I don't want her situation to go from bad to worse. I offered to help her, but she wouldn't take anything from me."

Unable to stop myself from touching her, I took Paige's hand. "She's as stubborn as you are," I told her with a grin. "She wants to work for what she has, and she doesn't want handouts."

"You really think this will help both of them?" she asked anxiously. "She was on the road, so I lost my connection with her earlier. I couldn't get a lot of information."

"Honestly...yes. It certainly can't hurt, and we're paying top dollar."

She squeezed my hand, and my heart kicked against my chest wall.

Paige finally visibly relaxed. "I hope you're right."

"Me, too."

She stood, her hand still in mine, as she said regretfully, "I have to get back to work. I guess we'll just have to see how it all works out. But I think you both should have told Dane what you were doing. He's an adult. He should be able to make his own choices."

Trace nodded. "Agreed. But he's also our brother."

"I know," Paige said softly.

"I'll go with you downstairs," I said eagerly, getting up to walk with her to the elevator.

"I'll see you at dinner next week," Trace reminded Paige.

She smiled. "I'll be there. I wouldn't miss Italian night. Pasta is my weakness, and I already know that Eva can make it better than any restaurant I've ever been to."

Trace and Paige parted amiably, and we walked hand-in-hand to the elevator. We stepped into one of the lifts that was open and empty.

I didn't miss the opportunity to wrap my arms around her and momentarily absorb the feel of her into my soul. "Everything will be okay," I promised her.

She put her hands on my shoulders and looked up at me with her beautiful blue-eyed stare. "I hope so. I do want Kenzie to be happy."

"And I want you to be happy," I countered.

"Oh, I am. Right now we're right back in the place where it all began."

So we were. In the very same elevator we'd rode up in on that fateful day when Paige had grabbed me by the balls and never let go.

I crowded her against the wall playfully. "Are you going to ask me to move?"

She smiled at me, and my heart damn near exploded from my chest.

"No," she said teasingly. "I don't think I will. I think I'd rather you kissed me."

"The smell of your hair still makes me hard," I admitted as I inhaled deeply after I buried my face into her thick, dark locks.

"And you still smell like sexy, hot male and butterscotch."

I decided I could live with that as I swooped down to capture her mouth, wanting to brand Paige Rutledge as mine forever.

Maybe we'd come full circle as we shared a passionate exchange in the very same elevator where we'd first met, but kissing her just got better and better.

How could I ever have known that the woman who got me hard for the first time in a long time would end up meaning everything to me?

I wrapped my arm around her waist as we exited the elevator on the ground floor, then stopped her in the lobby, which was considerably more crowded than it had ever been those several times she'd rejected me.

"Have dinner with me tonight?" I asked teasingly. But maybe I just wanted the satisfaction of hearing her say 'yes' this time.

She appeared to catch my meaning and smiled up at me. "Why, yes, Mr. Walker, I think I will."

"About damn time," I grumbled as I kissed her on the forehead.

I decided I really *did* want to hear her say she was willing to be with me, because my heart still hammered with elation, even though she was wearing my ring.

I grinned like a fool as I walked her to her car, feeling like the luckiest bastard in the world.

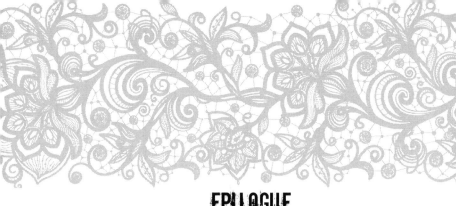

EPILOGUE

Paige

A FEW WEEKS LATER...

"It's finally over," I told Sebastian as we watched the news report that Justin Talmage was being charged with several serious felony charges in Julie's case.

"He's just been charged and is being held in jail," he said cautiously as he turned off the TV.

We were in our usual position, my back plastered against his front as we laid on the couch to catch the news.

I shook my head. "It really *is* over. These are charges his daddy can't buy him out of, and there's hard evidence. Plus, women are coming out of the woodwork to tell their stories about him. I can't believe he's gotten away with what he's been doing for so long. So many women."

So far, the count of previous victims was fifteen, none of them ever in a position to challenge Talmage, or were just too afraid to do it. Although none of them had any more evidence than I did, Julie's case was so strong that Justin would be put away for a long time. I'd be there for the trial and to watch that happen.

The thought brought me nothing but relief. Julie was strong, and currently in counseling. She had the support of her family and her boyfriend, so she wasn't going to break for any reason.

"He's not as well-known here as he is on the East Coast," Sebastian considered aloud. "So that will help."

"I'm sorry about Julie, but I'm glad she's alive and that Justin will finally get what he deserves this time," I said sleepily.

"He deserves to be six feet under," Sebastian grumbled.

I smiled. "I'm an attorney. I can't agree with that."

"You don't have to," Sebastian said as he tightened his arms around my waist. "I can hate the bastard that much all by myself."

"I hate him, too," I said calmly. "But what he did doesn't rule my life anymore. He never did deserve that kind of power."

I'd spoken to several of the women who'd been Justin's victims. Some of them had moved on better than others. But I was determined that he'd never be able to take away my power again.

I laughed.

I loved.

I'd forgiven my parents and they'd forgiven me.

I was working the job of my dreams, something I was passionate about.

Most importantly, I had Sebastian Walker, the man who had taught me that sex wasn't a useless or bad thing. In fact, it was downright orgasmic.

"I love you, Paige. You're so damn brave after everything he did to you."

"I'm not," I argued, wiggling to turn around to face him. "You made me brave, Sebastian. I was pretty much stuck until you set me free."

"You would have figured it out," he answered with certainty.

Would I have recognized what Sebastian had seen almost immediately? I'd like to think I would have realized I was running away from life, cocooning myself to stay safe. "I'm glad it happened this way. I'd rather it was you."

"We've helped each other, baby. That's what love is all about," Sebastian drawled lazily.

I sigh as I looked into his dark, beautiful eyes, seeing his love for me in his gaze. "I think I owe you." I didn't think I'd done nearly as much for him as he'd done for me.

He shook his head. "You love me. That's pretty damn extraordinary."

I smiled at him. "You're easy to love."

He grinned. "What woman could love an ex-player?"

"Me," I stated simply. "Very easily."

I understood Sebastian, just like he comprehended my actions.

"That's why you're mine, sweetheart. You sealed your own fate."

"I know," I said with a sigh, wrapping my arms around his neck. "I did good."

He laughed wickedly. "See, to my way of thinking, that's where you fucked up. You actually believe I'm a good guy, even though I was an asshole for a very long time. But it's too late. You're stuck with me. I'm never letting you go."

His arms grew tighter, and although I knew he was joking, there was a very serious timbre in his voice.

I didn't care about Sebastian's past. He had been growing up and struggling with major issues. All that mattered was who he was now, and the fact that he'd rejoined life with a passionate nature that rocked my world.

Sebastian was possessive, but I actually loved that part of him, and I wouldn't want him any other way. "I'm not exactly struggling to get away."

I rubbed my body against him like a cat.

"You're asking for trouble," he growled.

"I know," I answered in a sultry voice.

"*Jesus.* I love you, woman," he rasped against my ear.

"I love you, too, Sebastian," I said with a happy sigh.

I forgot about everything else in the world except the man I loved as he rose from the couch and took me with him. I knew he was going to prove just how much he loved me, and my body trembled with longing as I wrapped my legs around his waist and forgot the rest of the world for a while and just let our love and need completely surround us.

Sebastian and I had waited so long to find each other, and we were eager to make up for the years of loneliness we'd both endured.

My parents and Trace had been right. When you find the right person...you just know it in your heart and in your gut.

Our meeting wasn't as perfect or as profound as I'd always dreamed it would be. But those were the dreams of a girl.

As a woman, my relationship with Sebastian was so much more than I ever dreamed it could be.

And when my fiancé took me to bed and loved me like no other man ever had, I realized that my reformed player was absolutely perfect.

~ *The End* ~

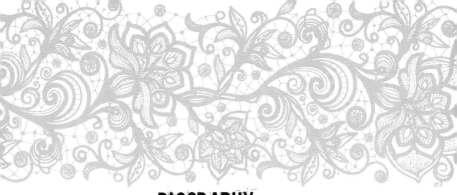

BIOGRAPHY

J.S. "Jan" Scott is a New York Times, Wall Street Journal and USA Today bestselling author of steamy romance. She's an avid reader of all types of books and literature. Writing what she loves to read, J.S. Scott writes both contemporary steamy romance stories and paranormal romance. They almost always feature an Alpha Male and have a happily ever after because she just can't seem to write them any other way! She lives in the beautiful Rocky Mountains with her husband and two very spoiled German Shepherds.

AUTHOR NOTE:

It's estimated that one in four college-aged women will experience date rape. Over eighty percent of college rape victims know or are acquainted with their attacker. I think those are pretty scary statistics. It can be an emotionally crippling, terrifying experience to be assaulted by a man you know, and many women are too embarrassed or frightened to report the event. Rape is rape, whether you know the male perpetrator or not. It's sexual activity without consent.

To avoid being a victim, always set your boundaries and your limits, and don't be afraid or pressured into sex. No means no. Never feel guilty about leaving an uncomfortable situation. Tell a friend where you're going and who you are with. Limit your intake of alcohol to one or two drinks. Never drink from community punch bowls, and never accept a drink from someone else. If you ever lose sight of your glass, don't finish it. Make sure you always have emergency money for a cab if you need to quickly leave a bad situation.

If something does happen, report it immediately. Make it possible for police to gather evidence by going straight to the authorities. It might be scary and hard to talk about immediately, but you might be able to save another woman from the same fate in the future.

Please don't be a statistic. Avoid situations where a date rape could easily occur, and please stay safe.

XXX ~ Jan

Please visit me at:

http://www.authorjsscott.com
http://www.facebook.com/authorjsscott
https://www.instagram.com/authorj.s.scott

You can write to me at
jsscott_author@hotmail.com

You can also tweet
@AuthorJSScott

Please sign up for my Newsletter for updates,
new releases and exclusive excerpts.

Books by J. S. Scott:

The Billionaire's Obsession Series:

The Billionaire's Obsession
Heart of The Billionaire
The Billionaire's Salvation
The Billionaire's Game
Billionaire Undone
Billionaire Unmasked
Billionaire Untamed
Billionaire Unbound
Billionaire Undaunted
Billionaire Unknown

The Sinclairs:

The Billionaire's Christmas
No Ordinary Billionaire
The Forbidden Billionaire
The Billionaire's Touch
The Billionaire's Voice

The Walker Brothers:

Release!
Player!

The Vampire Coalition Series:

The Vampire Coalition: The Complete Collection
Ethan's Mate
Rory's Mate
Nathan's Mate
Liam's Mate
Daric's Mate

The Sentinel Demons:

The Sentinel Demons: The Complete Collection
A Dangerous Bargain
A Dangerous Hunger
A Dangerous Fury
A Dangerous Demon King

The Curve Collection: Big Girls And Bad Boys
The Changeling Encounters Collection

Printed in Great Britain
by Amazon